DAY

By Michael Cunningham

DAY

MICHAEL CUNNINGHAM

4th ESTATE • *London*

4th Estate
An imprint of HarperCollins*Publishers*
1 London Bridge Street
London SE1 9GF

www.4thestate.co.uk

HarperCollins*Publishers*
Macken House, 39/40 Mayor Street Upper,
Dublin 1, D01 C9W8, Ireland

First published in Great Britain in 2024 by 4th Estate
First published in the US in 2024 by Random House

2 4 6 8 10 9 7 5 3 1

Epigraph quotation from *Selected Poems* by Anna Akhmatova published by
Harvill Press, translated by D.M. Thomas. Copyright © D.M. Thomas, 1988.
Reprinted by permission of Penguin Books Limited.

Book design by Ralph Fowler

A catalogue record for this book is
available from the British Library

ISBN 978-0-00-863756-9

FICTION

Printed and bound in India by Thomson Press India Ltd

This book is for Frances Coady

Rising from the past, my shadow
Comes silently to meet me.

—Anna Akhmatova

April 5, 2019

Morning

This early, the East River takes on a thin layer of translucence, a bright steely skin that appears to float over the river itself as the water turns from its nocturnal black to the opaque deep green of the approaching day. The lights on the Brooklyn Bridge go pale against the sky. A man pulls up the metal shutter of his shoe repair shop. A young woman, ponytailed, jogs past a middle-aged man who, wearing a little black dress and combat boots, is finally returning home. The occasional lit-up window is exactly as bright as the quarter moon.

Isabel, who has not slept, stands at her bedroom window, wearing an XXL T-shirt that reaches to the middle of her thighs. The ponytailed woman jogs past the man in the dress as he fits his key into the lock of his lobby door. The shoe repair man pulls up the steel grate, preparing to open his shop. Why does he open so early, who could possibly need shoes repaired at five A.M.?

The first tentative signs of spring have arrived. The tree in front of Isabel's building (a silver maple, which, according to Google, is "messy and shallow-rooted") has produced hard little buds that will soon burst into five-pronged leaves, unremarkable until a strong enough wind flutters up their silver undersides. On a windowsill across the street, a bouquet of daffodils stands in a water glass. The winter light which has, for months, been still and pale, seems to have quickened, as if the molecules of the air itself are newly activated.

Early April in Brooklyn might be spring by the calendar, but true spring—its hints of greenness, its awakening of stems and shoots—is weeks away. The buds on the tree are still just tight little nodes, waiting to crack open. The daffodils in the window across the street mean only that you can buy them at the corner market, that they've started arriving from wherever it is they grow.

Isabel turns from her own window to check on Dan, who is still deeply asleep, breathing heavily, as childlike in slumber as a forty-year-old man could possibly be, his mouth slackly open, his white-blond hair bright in the shadowy room.

Imagine being able to sleep like that. Isabel begrudges Dan his talent for slumber but is grateful for it, too. During the hours Dan and the kids are asleep, she—for whom sleep is rarely more than a skittish, dream-flecked attempt at sleep—might as well be alone in the apartment, immersed in her own waking dream of nightly solitude, marked only by the green LED numerals on the kitchen clock.

She sees the owl when she turns back to the window. It seems, at first, like an outgrowth of the tree branch on which it roosts. Its feathers are an almost perfect match for the dusky, variegated gray-brown of the bark. Isabel might not have seen the owl at all were it not for its eyes, two black-and-gold disks no bigger than dimes, blazingly attentive, utterly un-human. It seems, momentarily, that the tree itself has chosen this moment to inform Isabel that it is sentient, and watchful. The owl, small, about the size of a gardening glove, seems at first to be looking at Isabel but, after Isabel has adjusted herself to its gaze, is clearly looking only in Isabel's vicinity, staring not only at her but at the room in which she stands—at the bedside table with its unlit lamp and its copy of last month's *Atlantic;* at the wall behind the table with its framed photograph of the kids, a professional black and white in which they are disquietingly innocent, docile-looking versions of themselves. The owl aims its unblinking feline eyes at everything on Isabel's side of the window glass, does not appear to distinguish between Isabel and the lamp and the photograph, does not comprehend or care that she is alive and the rest of it is not. She and the owl remain briefly in place, eyes locked, before the owl flies away, so effortlessly that it seems not to beat its wings at all but merely to consent to flight. It arcs up, and vanishes. There is, in its departure, a sense of abdication, as if its presence in the tree outside the window had been a mistake, an unintended opening in the fabric of the possible, quickly and efficiently rectified. The owl seems already to have been a waking dream of Isabel's, which would make sense, given that she was not able to sleep at all last night (she can usually manage a few hours), that another day's difficulties are about to roll in (Robbie still hasn't found another place to live, Derrick isn't likely to give up on the reshoot), and that soon she'll be compelled to join it all, to muster the most convincing possible manifestation of herself, a person who can do everything that's required of her.

The owl has disappeared. The jogger has jogged on. The man in the dress has gone into his building. There's only the shoe repair man, who has turned on the shop's fluorescent light, a light that does not radiate from behind the glass of the shop's window, does not offer any added illumination to the street. Isabel has no idea whether the shoe repair man, to whom she has never spoken (she has her shoes fixed in midtown), opens so early because he's escaping some ongoing domestic struggle or if he's merely eager to revisit his rectangle of light, because he takes pleasure in turning on the blue neon sign that says SHOE HOSPITAL (Isabel really should start taking her shoes to him, if only because he thinks of his shop as a shoe hospital) and in reactivating the three-foot-tall mannequin in the window, a sun-bleached ... fox, raccoon? ... that sits at a cobbler's bench, raising and lowering a miniature hammer, which, now that the shoe repair man has switched it on again, now that the SHOE HOSPITAL sign blazes gas-blue and the animal has resumed its labors, will do as an announcement of the start of the day.

f Wolfe were real, he'd be the elusive figure at the heart of the story. He'd be the animated, friends-encircled guy you fail to meet at a party, the athletic-looking stranger glimpsed as he strides off the B train, the prince whose kiss might fix everything if he were able to find you, comatose in your glass casket, deep in the woods.

Wolfe's 3,407 followers all feel more or less the same about him. He's one of those guys who appear not only to be getting what they want but to want what they're getting. Wolfe's followers Like his chronicle of his own dailiness. They Like his sable-stubbled, off-center beauty. He's both fabulous and obtainable, a regular guy with the volume turned up a little, the lights on full. He's the handsome-ish man who'll follow through, who'll stick around, who sees it in you, that . . . youness that seems to escape the notice of others, or fails to hold their interest, over time.

Wolfe is fascinated by your gorgeousness of person. He's thirtyish. He's ready to commit. He doesn't need to be the prettiest person in the room, though there's nothing he can do about the fact that, more often than not, he's the most magnetic. He emanates. And yet, he's innocent of vanity. He's hot for now—he benches two hundred, has no idea about the way water beads in his curls when he steps out of the shower, doesn't clock the boys who clock his pecs and abs in the locker room—

and nurtures no pre-regrets about the future, when he'll be nearsighted, a few pounds overweight, a good doctor who attends faithfully to his patients while awaiting tonight with you, just you, which is all he desires, all he needs.

His followers Like it that he's a pediatrician, one year to go on his residency, working at a community clinic. They Like that he lives in Brooklyn with his roommate, Lyla, and with Arlette, their recently adopted beagle-and-whatever mix. They Like the implication, never directly stated, that he's had a few boyfriends who didn't quite work out and that he's waiting now to fall in love but is in no particular hurry about it. He is cheerfully virginal, for all the beds he's been in and out of. It's impossible to say how many of his followers are in love with him, how many of them are convinced that, were they to meet, they'd prove to be the person for whom Wolfe is so patiently waiting.

That's a too-large question for this early in the morning, when Robbie still has to read more than a dozen essays by the members of his sixth-grade history class about how the Indigenous people may have felt when Columbus sailed in.

Thinking about Wolfe's first post of the day, Robbie brews the coffee, pops a Paxil and an Adderall, pauses to orient himself under the square of brightening gray sky that shines through the kitchen skylight, a jerry-built addition on the part of some previous resident. It does admit more light into the attic apartment, but it also leaks, despite every effort to seal it. Even now a single droplet of water, bright as the sky itself, trembles at the skylight's lower left-hand corner. Dew, condensation, whatever. It hasn't rained in weeks.

The whole apartment is subject to incursions by water: the

bathroom faucet that will not stop dripping; the line of dark inundation that collects, even in the lightest of rains, on the floor under the sliding glass door, which offers access to the fire escape and was surely the work of the same well-intended, if unskilled, former occupant. If Robbie were more prone to morbid romanticism, he might consider all this unstoppable seepage to be a vestige of the grief suffered by the attic's original inhabitants, who would have been Irish girls come to America in flight from the famine only to find themselves vying for jobs as housemaids—girls who'd been sought after in Dublin, girls of whom it had been said, *In another few years, she'll have her pick*. Girls who were now expected to be grateful for two damp rooms in the attic of a row house in Brooklyn.

Robbie is the latest in a line of people who, unlike the long-dead Irish girls, have considered this cramped, dank warren to be a lucky break. Which of his more recent predecessors was the optimist who, in an attempt to admit light, did not fully anticipate the rain and sleet of Brooklyn winters? Who else (it has to have been someone else) painted the place a murky orange-brown that's been painted over in white but that remains, like the saddest possible haunting, on the bit of wall behind the cabinet under the kitchen sink. Did that denizen come before or after the one who punched the leaky skylight into the ceiling?

And now here's Robbie, a schoolteacher who makes sixty grand and survives in a New York where you can't rent anything livable for less than three thousand, minimum, a New York where, if you're lucky, your sister bought the top two floors of a brownstone and offered you the attic for less than she pays on the mortgage.

You're lucky until your luck expires. You're lucky until your sister wants the apartment back.

It's time for you to create your own luck, then.

The Adderall is kicking in, which is fortunate, given that last night Robbie watched five episodes of *Fleabag* instead of reading the remaining essays, still piled on the kitchen table.

He's able to put off reading the essays because the school is closed for a few hours this morning while its walls are tested for asbestos. It's widely held that the asbestos was removed from the walls more than twenty years ago, but someone recently noticed that any record of the removal seems to be missing from the files, along with all other records of the year 1998, and so a team of people in what Robbie imagines to be hazmat suits are drilling into the walls for asbestos that probably isn't there, unless the walls were not really checked—unless the "missing" records never existed in the first place, and everyone has merely assumed it was taken care of.

As Robbie takes an essay from the top of the stack, he does his best to delay worrying about whether he and his students have been sucking invisible black fishhooks into their lungs every Monday through Friday.

He's picked up Sonia Thomas's essay. Sonia is a contemplative red-haired girl whose tale of having been adopted from Romania at the age of seven is, apparently, fictitious, offered as the story of her origin for reasons no one comprehends and no one has yet inquired about.

Her essay's opening line: "We thought that that man in the big boat was bringing us magic."

Robbie puts the essay down. He's not ready yet. He considers eating a Cheeto. He's struck by that which he, which most people, know already: there must be some intricate series of barely visible connections, a subterranean network that connects those ships appearing on the horizon to slave auctions, to Lewis and Clark first beholding the Missouri River, the War to End All Wars, the Chicago World's Fair, the Depression and the New Deal, another war, the rocket belts we were supposed to be wearing by now, random shootings in supposedly undangerous places (schools and movie theaters, village greens, the list goes on) as people die trying to cross a border into a land where they hope they'll be able to be servants or gardeners, as ever more inhabitable planets show up at unfathomable distances, as Robbie himself worries over losing the apartment that once imprisoned those long-dead Irish girls.

He hopes neither his nor Sonia's lungs are studded with microscopic carcinogenic hooks. He wonders if he should try getting back with Oliver. He wonders if he's brought about his own doom by teaching in a zero-budget public school where it's all too possible that tests for asbestos were never really conducted. He wonders if turning down medical school was a mistake, after all. He wonders if he should reconsider some of the apartments he's seen already. What about the one-bedroom in Bushwick, which had high ceilings but only that single porthole of a window? Was he too hasty in rejecting the "mini-loft" (so advertised) because it shared a bathroom with the mini-loft next door?

Maybe Wolfe needs to embark on some kind of adventure. Get away for a while, hit the road. Wolfe lives, after all, at the eastern edge of a vast continent host to farmhouses afloat on seas of corn, to mountains and forests and all-night diners where someone will call you honey as they refill your coffee mug. His followers must want him to go out into all that. Some of them, at least, must want to know that he's out there, in motion. He might cross paths with you. You might prove to be the one he's been waiting for, all this time.

Who isn't hoping for a magician to arrive on their shore?

When Robbie starts downstairs, from his place to Isabel and Dan's, he finds Isabel on the stairs, sitting with her knees pressed together and her arms wrapped around her knees, as if to make the smallest possible package of herself.

"Good morning," he says. From two treads above, the top of her head is her most prominent feature. Her hair is still sleep-tangled, the part gone ragged, showing white zigzags of scalp.

Robbie and Isabel do not much resemble each other. Isabel inherited their mother's bright gray eyes under heavy brows, along with her bony jut of nose, which, in Isabel, is at commanding odds with the pugilistic jaw inherited from neither parent. She learned early on that if so-called beauty resided precariously in her, ferocity would do instead. *I will be sought after, I will have boyfriends, I'll be president of the senior class.* She has, for as long as Robbie can remember, laid claim to her own singularity simply because she looks so unapologetically like herself.

In Robbie, their mother's raptorish features—her aspect of a falcon transformed into a woman, someone watchful and hard-bargaining—were leavened by their father's Anglo-Irish symmetry: his modesty of nose and chin, his milk-chocolate-colored eyes, his undangerous affability.

In high school Isabel cut like a blade through the foolishness of others, the jocks and the homecoming queens. Robbie was the less robust, the one with the delicate heart. There were the glasses he wore from the age of five (he'd rather not dwell on those baby-blue contacts he wore for a year, at twenty). Robbie was always pensive and inward (thanks, Mom, for calling it "brooding," like Heathcliff, even if you intended to imply that Robbie was no Heathcliff and should start making more efforts in that general direction). Robbie was cripplingly aware of the insults that were genuinely intended by others and, worse, the insults he could imagine but was unable to hear. Robbie wanted desperately to be loved, which, as he sees in retrospect, was an effective method for guaranteeing that love would be almost universally withheld by everyone except the members of his family.

"Good morning," Isabel says.

"Here it is. Morning."

"How are the Columbus essays going?"

"So far, there are six who think of him as a vicious invader, three who think he invented America, and that that was a good idea. One from a kid who seems to think the assignment was about what Columbus was wearing."

"What was he wearing?"

"Some kind of robe. And what sounds like a tiara on his head."

"Nice."

"It is. And yet."

"And yet."

"Lately I've been thinking about how much longer I can do this. I mean, I've been feeling more exhausted by it all. You have no idea what it's like to be in a *room* with them, every day."

"I know this. You know I know this, right?"

"Yeah, sure. But. Even the past week or two—"

She says, "I have to ask. Are you extra exhausted because you're moving out?"

"I'm going to ask you one more time not to feel guilty about this."

"Are you sorry about medical school?"

"No. I'm not sorry about med school," he says. "And really, almost every other teacher seems to wish they'd done something else. Except Myrna."

"Who's unqualified to teach. Or, I suppose, do much of anything."

"She should at least get a new wig."

Isabel says, "I've been thinking more about Dad lately. Whatever Dr. Meer says about how he's doing."

"Well, yeah, Dr. Meer—"

"Did Dad tell you Dr. Meer mentioned taking a trip to Lourdes? Like, why not take a shot at miraculous intervention."

"Which would probably be about as good a shot as Dr. Meer. Did you happen to notice that all the magazines in his waiting room are at least a year old? Did you notice the bowl of candy corn? From Halloween?"

"This is serious," she says. "Do you think you could take it seriously?"

"Do you think I'm *not* taking it seriously?"

"No," she says. "I know you are. Is there really a bowl of candy corn in his office? Maybe I've just refused to notice it."

"Listen."

"I'm listening. I'm absolutely listening."

"I didn't *not* go to med school because Dad wanted me to,"

he says. "I would not be the better doctor who could take care of him now. Isn't that a long-established fact?"

"You know how I feel about facts."

"And maybe going to Lourdes isn't the worst idea. It'd get Dad out of the house."

"I saw an owl this morning," she says. "In the tree."

"The shitty tree in front of the building?"

"Uh-huh."

"Not possible."

"There are owls in Central Park."

"That's Central Park," he says.

"All right. I dreamt that I saw an owl this morning. Did you post anything for Wolfe yet?"

Wolfe is, in a sense, an adult incarnation of the older brother the two of them made up when they were children—the big brother who defended them, who feared nothing and no one, who knew the languages of animals.

Isabel and Robbie called their imaginary brother Wolf. Robbie has never confessed that until he was six, he'd thought the boy's name was Woof.

"Not yet," he says. "I'm too deep in Christopher Columbus."

"I like the idea of Columbus in a tiara."

Robbie sits beside her on the third tread. He's aware of her morning scent, pre-shower. A melony freshness, a hint of old flowers. They grew up with each other's essences, but it's been a while since Robbie has caught her so early, unwashed. He can't help inhaling.

He says, "I'm looking at a place in Washington Heights this afternoon. It seems there's a view of the river."

"It'd be nice to have a view of the river. As opposed to the shitty tree and the Shoe Hospital."

"I should have done this a while ago."

She says, "Last night, Violet asked me what Nathan's penis is for."

"What did you tell her?"

"That boys are different."

"Did that answer the question?"

"No. She was asking about its actual purpose."

"That's our girl. Five years old, and she's ready for the *facts*."

"Let's say it was a reminder that they're way too old to be sharing a room. I don't know how Dan and I let it go this long. We're such shitty parents."

"No. You're parents who've only got two bedrooms."

"I keep thinking about that house in the country we were going to buy," she says.

"We were kids."

"We were going to have a dozen rooms, and a vegetable garden, and three or four dogs."

"That was Ms. Manley's idea," he says. "You got it from her, and I got it from you."

"She was the best fifth-grade teacher. Every child should have a hippie teacher."

"With a romantic relationship to reality."

"But people do move to the country. There are all those houses up there, at what I hear are reasonable prices."

"And the next-nearest gay person would be, like, thirty miles away."

"I'm sorry about Oliver."

"Oliver would never have wanted to move to the country."

Isabel says, "Why don't we give Wolfe a house upstate?"

"I don't know. Do we want that, for him?"

"Why not? He works so hard."

"He's needed by the children at the clinic."

Isabel punches Robbie's shoulder, playfully, as she's been doing since . . . he can't remember a time she wasn't doing it. It is, has always been, a comradely gesture, but it is (has always been) delivered with sufficient force to be fleetingly painful, to suggest that camaraderie can contain an implication of rage.

She says, "I can't believe you have him taking care of sick children."

"He doesn't dwell on it. He hardly ever even mentions it."

"You would have been a good doctor."

"Hey," he says, "it's not as if I'm a bad teacher. I'm just having one of those mornings. I blame it on Christopher Columbus."

"You didn't *want* to go to medical school. You didn't start teaching elementary school only to spite Dad."

"Then again, who doesn't like the simpler story?"

"Do you think Wolfe gets along with his father?" she says.

"Wolfe is just some postings on Instagram. We're making him up as we go along. He's not a person. He's barely even the idea of a person."

"Am I getting bossy?"

"Maybe slightly."

"Remember when I ate your whole birthday cake?"

"You were four. I was two. I don't even remember this."

"Mom told the story about a hundred times. It was the official house story about what we were like when we were kids."

"Why are you thinking about this now?"

"I guess because I'm someone who eats other people's birthday cakes. I'm evicting my brother. Things at work get stupider and stupider, and I go along with it."

"How stupid is it right now?"

"Today I have to talk Derrick out of reshooting the Astoria piece, on zero budget. And there are some kind of rumblings about the queer families story. Which have yet to be revealed."

"How about if I go down and check on Dan and the kids?"

"Would you? I wouldn't mind a few more minutes alone here. There's this neither-here-nor-there thing about sitting on the stairs."

"Everything will be okay."

"Yes. Absolutely. Everything will be okay."

sabel and Dan's apartment was almost half finished when the children arrived and set about undoing it. Before Nathan was born—more than a year sooner than planned—Isabel and Dan had had the time and money to paint the living room walls an opalescent gray, to refinish the floors from glossy oak to an ebony-tinged matte brown so dark it verges on black, to buy the Italian armchair and the impeccably weathered nineteenth-century bookcases that had found their way to Brooklyn from Buenos Aires. But Nathan's birth put a halt to renovations, and before Nathan turned five—when his destructive capabilities finally seemed containable, when Isabel and Dan had started shopping for new sofas and lamps—Violet's conception deferred, for at least the next few years, any purchase of any consequence.

And so Isabel and Dan and the kids still live in the too-small apartment that was intended to be temporary, their starter apartment before real estate prices went into the stratosphere, before Dan and Isabel's idea about eventually buying the ground-floor apartment was forestalled by the impossibly long lives of the ancient twins who'd lived there since before World War II and was then canceled outright when the twins were removed to assisted living and the ground-floor apartment sold immediately to someone who arrived with a suitcase filled with a million and a half in cash, so his son would have a place to stay during the summers, when he came home from Yale.

The living room in which Isabel and Dan still live remains suspended in its neither-here-nor-there condition. Here, still, is the mocha-colored sofa Isabel bought from a thrift shop, years ago. Here is the patchy Guatemalan rug from Dan's old place on Avenue B, and the massive "Spanish-style" coffee table, like a pirate ship moored in the middle of the room, given by Isabel and Robbie's father in a fit of what he called downsizing after their mother died but which has proven, over time, to mean that he merely intends to live in an ongoing state of mourning, with fewer furnishings and brighter lights. He has not, since he became a widower, bought a lightbulb less than 75 watts, as if he needs the brightest possible light in order to properly see his own solitude.

Isabel and Robbie should call him; it's been a while.

In the living room, Robbie searches for an image from Wolfe's folder (#wolfe_man).

Wolfe is not some hyperbolic, studly fantasy. Wolfe's decently handsome, dark-eyed face is that of a stranger lifted from Depositphotos. His roommate, Lyla, is, in reality, an effortlessly fashionable Black woman whose Instagram name is Galatea2.2. His apartment is an amalgam of three different places. His dog was recently adopted from a shelter by someone called Inezhere.

Robbie hopes he's not doing harm, not only by pilfering the posted photos of strangers (he's amazed that he hasn't gotten caught yet) but by rearranging them into someone who doesn't exist. Or, rather, who exists as a garnering of other people's specifics.

The Frankenstein association is inevitable.

Wolfe, however, is the idea of a person, not a violation of formerly living tissue. He's not going to come to life mortified, lost, desperate for connection. He's not going to drift away on an iceberg into a frigid sea. He's a fantasy—a sweet and relatively minor one—shared (as it turns out) by 3,407 others.

There can't be any harm in that, can there?

Robbie chooses a photo, sends off today's first post:

Image: A field in Vermont, or possibly New Hampshire. Photos like this are easy to find. Robbie's got a half dozen or more in the folder already. This one depicts an expanse of blindingly green grass presided over by a tree sprouting thumbnail-sized white blossoms. In the foreground, the upper right-hand corner of the side mirror of the car from which somebody called Horsefeather took the photograph. It must be from another year, it's too early for this much greenness and blossoming so far north, but Robbie doesn't worry about verisimilitude. Wolfe is a fictitious person who lives in a fictitious world of shifting time and precarious seasons. His followers seem not to notice, or to mind. Robbie, in collecting images for Wolfe, must have anticipated some pastoral release for him, liberation from his own happiness, even if the scenes of his escape are not always technically possible.

Caption: Road trip! One day only. It's all crazy with spring here couldn't miss that.

It's greeted immediately with eleven Likes.

Dan stands at the kitchen counter, cracking an egg into a bowl. He is, as always, true to type: the former rock and roller as portly, magisterial forty-year-old, a missing figure in art. The Greeks favored muscular middle age for men, warriors grown all the more formidable as they aged. It seems, after that, that the depiction of middle-aged men skipped the intervening centuries (even Michelangelo preferred younger guys) and went directly from their heroic Greek incarnations to the rancid pink man-cakes of Francis Bacon.

A figure like Dan is missing from the collective agreement about male comeliness: the guy grown stocky and slightly, voluptuously soft, a figure more devoted to affection than to fighting, more troubled by systems and savings than the gladiatorial ring; a man taking his first steps in the general direction of mortality, which, as far as Robbie is concerned, requires more fortitude than the conviction that, with enough exercise and cosmetic work, you can keep looking like you're thirty-eight until your eightieth birthday.

Dan wears gray sweatpants and an ancient Ramones T-shirt. A circle of unconcealed scalp offers itself from the back of his platinum head—peroxide is his only remaining insistence on his former life. Who could blame him for wanting to retain a vestige of his youthful magnificence? How does anyone recover from having looked, at age twenty, like a seraph out of Botticelli?

Dan's hair aside, though, he's grown dutiful, prone to unwavering devotions. He's had the anger leached out of him by his own jokingly hardy embrace of the disappointments, along with his hopes for a future that still lies ahead. He cracks the egg with finesse and precision.

"Morning, Robbie," he says. His voice has permanently dropped by half an octave after all those years of smoking, of singing into the foggy lights of clubs.

"Hey, Danny."

Robbie butts his head into Dan's meaty shoulder. "How you doing?" Dan asks.

"Fine. Okay. Hey, it's finally Friday."

That was a little insensitive, wasn't it? If weekends mean freedom for Robbie they mean, for Dan, that the kids are home from school all day, and Isabel will be on her laptop much of the time (with more than a third of the staff gone, she works seven days a week).

Robbie wonders if his own imminent departure is rendering him more prone to tiny insults, or merely more aware of the tiny insults he's always lobbed at Dan. Dan who is a mensch, Dan who is ardently loved, Dan who has become, no denying it, a figure of pathos.

"Is Isabel all right?" he asks.

"Yep. Just needs a little quiet."

"I've got a new song. I was up most of the night with it."

"Are the kids still in their room?"

"Yep," Dan says. "Violet's getting dressed. Nathan is, well, I don't exactly know what Nathan is doing."

"I'll go move things along. You know I've got this morning off, right?"

"I guess I do. Remind me."

"Some sort of crew is coming to the school, to run tests for asbestos."

"I thought they got rid of all the asbestos."

"Probably. But they can't rule it out. They're not sure if anybody ever checked. The records are ... picture cardboard boxes in a basement that got flooded in Hurricane Sandy."

"So you get the morning off, then."

"I'll go round up the kids."

"Love you, man."

"Love you, too."

A couple of decades ago, when Dan and Isabel were debating about marriage (she had doubts), Dan took Robbie, age seventeen, on a road trip to see the World's Largest Ball of Twine, in the hope that Isabel could be nudged along if Dan brought her little brother over to his side. On his more nostalgic days, Robbie considers the trip to have been the time of his life. Dan, twenty, at the wheel of his thirdhand Buick Skylark, all dark-gold curls and sinewy arms, singing along to "Sweet Thing" as the farms of Pennsylvania and Ohio spread around them. Dan was all Robbie meant by the word "beautiful." Ever after, Robbie and Dan have told the story about driving all the way to Kansas to see what proved to be only the world's *second*-largest ball of twine, the largest being in Minnesota; about how the kindly, balding woman on duty that day proved unable to offer further details about the plaque's assertion that although this ball of twine was not in fact the largest, it was the only one that allowed visitors to get close enough to smell it. The woman merely smiled ruefully when Dan inquired about the benefits of smelling it. She offered instead an account of various controversies, among them the question of sisal versus plastic twine, and the debate over whether the term "largest" should apply to dimensions or to weight.

That's where the story ends. With Dan and Robbie, disappointed by the absence of a souvenir shop, headed home again in the Skylark, which would break down in Reading, Pennsylvania, where they'd spend the night in an ancient motel while a slightly dubious mechanic wired the engine back together, with the reluctant admission that it would probably, at least, get them home again.

If Robbie were able to invent the past as freely as he's inventing Wolfe, the story would continue. He and Dan would have kept driving after they'd seen the ball of twine, headed not back east but west, all the way to California, and it may have been somewhere halfway through Colorado when Dan realized he was not in love with Isabel after all but with her brother, a boy who'd bemoan the dearth of ball-of-twine T-shirts and refrigerator magnets, who'd play "Sweet Thing" over and over and over and sing along to it, who'd never mention any of Dan's less presentable habits (not even the flicking-his-thumbs thing), who'd never be impatient or jealous, who loved this Dan, precisely this person, and had no suggestions of any kind about ways in which Dan might improve himself. Robbie and Dan might have been living in Venice Beach ever since. On their anniversary they'd always go back to see the world's second-largest ball of twine. They'd never go to Minnesota to see the largest one.

sabel envisions herself sitting here on the stairs for years to come. She could be a figure in a European movie: the Woman on the Stairs. A woman paralyzed by her own selfishness and triviality, a woman who knew she should love her life more than she did but couldn't seem to love her life beyond a few odd inconsequential incidents. She's seen an owl where there could not reasonably have been an owl and, knowing that owls must symbolize some sort of misfortune—screech and talons descending from what had seemed a balmy night sky—has found that she can go neither up nor down the stairs. And so, here she is.

She'd remain here, indifferent to all pleas and exhortations. She'd be here as her children grew older, as they learned to pass her on their way to and from home with a quick *Good morning, Momma* or *Good night, Momma*. She'd remain here after the children were grown, after her family moved away and a new family took their place. The new family would have been informed that the apartment was underpriced because they'd be compelled to agree to the presence of the Woman on the Stairs. They'd walk around her, generally politely, though their own children would, every now and then, shout *Hello* into her ear, until they tired of it as she failed, consistently, to react. She'd grow invisible to the new family. They would sometimes brush against her accidently or smack her on the

head with a bag of groceries, but as the first of their apologies
went as unremarked as did the children's imprecations, they'd
come to refer to her only when they had guests, to whom they'd
say, in muted tones, *Sorry, but she came with the place, we paid
almost nothing for it, and, well, there's not much we can do.*

Nathan and Violet's room is still the nursery Isabel exactingly constructed during her Perfect Mother Days, when Nathan was a thumb-sized curl in her uterus and Violet was waiting wherever the not-yet-conceived might wait. The walls are still papered with images of the planets and the constellations, bearing their names: Mars, Venus, Saturn; Andromeda, Cygnus, the Pleiades (clustered unfortunately close to the light switch). Isabel chose the cosmos over whimsy, winced at circus animals and candy stripes, which has made it easier, now that Violet is five and Nathan is ten, to maintain that they are not yet too old to share a room, since it's devoted to Ursa Major and Orion rather than lollipops and clowns. Soon Nathan will move to Robbie's place upstairs. Maybe he'll be the one who's finally able to fix the leaky skylight.

Robbie stands in the children's doorway, unobserved.

Violet poses in front of the mirror, admiring her own reflection. Nathan sits on his bed, already dressed, wearing his uniform: tight jeans and gray hoodie. He worries about eccentricity, in any form.

"Hey, mutants," Robbie calls.

They squeal (Nathan, as Robbie knows, immediately wishes he hadn't), and run to him. Violet wraps her skinny arms around Robbie's thighs; Nathan extends his fist for a bump.

"Hello hello hello," Violet says.

"Good morning, sweetheart."

Robbie strokes her hair with one hand, returns Nathan's fist bump with the other. "Hey, dude," Nathan says.

"Hey, Mary," Robbie replies. "Give us a squeeze."

Nathan moves in to hug Robbie, which causes Nathan to bump Violet's head with his elbow, which causes her to yelp in pain at approximately ten times the appropriate volume.

"Gimme a break," says Nathan.

"You hit my *head*."

"I *touched* your head. Don't be a drama queen."

"Say you're sorry," Violet says.

"I'm not sorry, because I didn't do anything."

"You *hit* me."

"Call 911."

Robbie, mired to his waist in quarreling children, says, "Stop. Okay?"

They don't stop. They can't. They're driven by an ancient filial wrath, stunning in its purity.

Violet says, "Nathan doesn't like my outfit."

"No, I said you look great if you were in a carnival."

"Robbie, do you like it?"

She steps back so that Robbie can see her more fully. She's wearing the aqua dress, a high princess number, with Juliet sleeves and a tulle skirt.

Robbie bought the dress for her a week ago. How had it failed to occur to him that she'd want to wear it as an everyday outfit?

"You look gorgeous," he says.

"Uh-*huh*," she replies, aimed at Nathan.

"But it might be a little much, for day," Robbie tells her.

She looks at him confusedly. She is coming into a world of hidden rules, which she can learn only by breaking them. Until recently the rules were often unfair, sometimes appallingly so, but clear.

She says, "For *today*?"

"A woman usually wears her fanciest clothes at night," Robbie says. "When the stars are out."

"So she looks more like a star."

"That's right."

"She wears her regular clothes during the day, and her fancy clothes at night."

"Exactly."

Violet picks up a tartan plaid skirt she's tossed, along with several others, onto the floor.

"Is this better? For today?"

"It's perfect."

"With this shirt?"

She proffers her current favorite, the T-shirt with the glittery peace sign. Robbie is not a fan of the shirt, but one correction is enough, for now.

"Perfect," he says.

"I can wear this today, and the dress tonight."

"Exactly."

"Do you think maybe tonight I could wear the dress *and* the shirt . . ."

"We'll discuss that later. Breakfast before fashion."

Violet nods compliantly but pulls away when Robbie reaches out to stroke her hair again. Underneath the lesson about day into evening he has been vaguely remonstrative, and she is vaguely angry at him. She is, in her current incarnation as a five-year-old girl, caught sometimes in impossible positions, when her need to be right collides with her need to have the mysteries explained.

Nathan has returned to his wide-legged posture on his bed,

playing a game on his iPhone. He was right about his sister's clothes. He knows already, at ten, to play it cool about the little victories.

For reasons that are mysterious to him, Robbie thinks of Violet as the more inevitable child, even though she's five years younger than Nathan. Nathan has, for as long as Robbie can remember, felt like a bit of an outsider—loved, welcomed, but here for now, until he vanishes into his own private future, whereas Violet is here, a member of the family, forever.

"Breakfast time, buddy," Robbie says.

As Robbie struggles to get them out of the bedroom, he asks himself: Has he helped to oppress Violet by encouraging her to obey a fundamental principle of fashion? Should he make sure Nathan knows that "drama queen" might not be the best phrase to use among his fifth-grade friends? Who knew, who could have anticipated—at that years-ago dinner, when Isabel first put her hand over her empty wineglass by way of announcing her pregnancy—that Robbie and Dan and Isabel were, all three of them, embarking on lives of adoration and exhaustion and ongoing doubt about whether (when) one of them will make the crucial mistake, the one the children will carry with them into the next century.

Then again, Robbie pictures himself, in his sixties, going out for drinks with Nathan, visiting from wherever he will have gone, jousting about politics. (*Nathan, do you really doubt that history is always about money?*) He envisions helping Violet pick out her prom dress. (*Why don't you try on the one without the sash?*) The very idea of that future (*Robbie, we've signed you up for Pilates, you need to stretch more*) is a lifeline he can follow straight to the horizon. It's been known to get him out of bed on the occasional bad morning.

Nathan leaves the bedroom first, with an air of barely patient resignation. Okay, sure, breakfast and school and everything, if it'll get Robbie off his back, although Nathan doesn't
need to eat breakfast (he lives on protein bars) and has only
idiots for teachers. He'll do it for Robbie.

Violet lingers, still unsure about abandoning the princess
dress. Robbie says to her, "You're not going to have the fish
sticks at lunch today, right?"

She fixes upon him a look of acute irritation, which Robbie
understands. Why would she be happy about the fact that he
checks the school lunch menu every morning and forbids her
anything too fatty or salty. But really, *fish sticks*? Bullets of fat
and salt. What are they thinking of, at her school?

He says, "You and I have big hearts. It's part of what's remarkable about us."

"It isn't fair," she tells him.

"We have to take care of our hearts. So they don't get too big
for our bodies."

"Because you gave me hypnoheart."

"Hypertension. It runs in the family. It's not my first choice
of things for you and me to have in common."

"I'm going to have one bite of a fish stick."

"One bite."

With a final look at the dress, which lies in a faintly irides-
cent heap on the floor, she agrees to go to breakfast.

One more morning obligation met. And now, along with
Robbie's domestic commitments, there are pictures to be posted
by his recently conceived friend, who was born online a couple
of months ago, after Oliver and Robbie broke up.

sabel is doing her eyes when Robbie walks into the bathroom.

"Uh, knock?" she says.

"I didn't know it was occupied. Is that Chanel?"

"I had a shopping emergency. Do you want to try it?"

"Sure."

They stand together before their reflections in the bathroom mirror. Robbie runs the eye shadow over his left eyelid, assesses his face in the mirror. The shadow is smoky but subtly so, fleshly, sultry. *You are a stunningly somnolent, unfrivolous person. There is nothing pink about you.*

Robbie says, "The place in Washington Heights sounds promising. They can't really say there's a view of the river if there's not a view of the river, right?"

"They all *sound* promising."

"Well, yeah, nobody mentions the fact that the place also overlooks the dumpsters behind a restaurant, or that the bedroom is in the basement."

"Do you think it's weird, giving Nathan his own place upstairs?"

"It's really an upstairs room that happens to be an apartment. Have you ever tried making dinner in that kitchen?"

"We're turning off the gas on the stove."

"And you keep the street door locked. No psychopaths can get in."

"I wish I didn't need this much reassurance."

"It's part of what I'm here for."

"You should be moving in with Oliver."

"Tell that to Oliver."

"Men are shits."

"Except Dan and me."

"Dan's a shit, too."

"You don't mean that."

"How are you talking to him about his *comeback*?"

"Uh, I'm encouraging it," Robbie says. "How else would I talk to him about it?"

"Mm."

"Are *you* talking to him about it?"

"No. I'm not," she says.

Isabel and Robbie agree about Dan's *comeback*. They keep no secrets (they believe that they keep no secrets), but there are a few shared concurrences about which they do not speak, many of which involve Dan. Dan hopes to reignite a lost period of glory spent as the opening act for bands no one ever heard of. He's coming back from a single album that didn't sell.

"I used to think married people talked about everything," Robbie says.

"I'm sure some of them do."

Isabel runs a brush over her eyelids, blinks appraisingly into the mirror. She has failed to be the woman who's always got a joke to tell during hard times, whose spur-of-the-moment dinner parties are legendary among their friends. Dan doesn't talk to her about that, either.

She says, "Exactly how far away is Washington Heights?"

"Forty-five minutes. Maybe an hour. Depending on the trains."

"That's pretty far."

"Yeah, but then again it's kind of semi-affordable."

"Maybe we really could get that country house."

"Ms. Manley could come and live with us," he says. "If she's, you know, still alive."

Isabel considers her face in the mirror.

"I guess it's that . . . as long as you're living upstairs, we seem sort of—"

"Communal?"

"That is such a Ms. Manley word."

He says, "It's not like I'm moving to Chicago or anything."

"It seems like you are."

"Are you all right?"

"Mm-hm," she says. "Mostly. It's just. Dan and I are in love with you. Never mind about the kids."

This is not a revelation. Robbie's in love with Isabel and Dan, too. Or, rather, he's in love with the restively joined singular creature they've become: Isabel's briskly knowing melancholia conjoined with Dan's unembarrassed optimism; her inner tumble of thwarted desires and his earnest if unreasonable expectations. Robbie's in love with the person they've created together—someone romantic, someone generous of heart, someone kind and gentle but wised-up and ironic, as well.

There's the fact, too, that Robbie may love them better than they're able to love each other. There's the fact that Isabel and Dan have been headed for heartbreak from the time they met, when Dan contended that Isabel's doubts were merely the skittishness of a girl who, as Dan put it, could sometimes be a little too smart for her own good, a girl who needed to accept the fact that Dan simply knew that this was *right;* after Isabel, having exhausted her own body of misgivings, decided to agree. How could anyone as sure, as sweet-smelling and roguishly courtly, as Dan Byrne be wrong?

But there's the fact that their element of mismatch, their underlayer of *not quite,* has not only persisted but grown. There's the fact that each of them considers Robbie to be their closest friend.

No one, however, until this morning, has spoken the words *in love.* Robbie can only hope Isabel means it when she says, *Dan and I are in love with you*—the "I" matters—and hope as well she knows that he too is in love with *both* of them, that he has no designs on Dan, not in the traditional sense. How sad and, worse, expected would it be, the gay brother lusting after his sister's husband?

He can't help wondering if Isabel, who claims always to tell him the absolute truth, is prevaricating on this one.

"You'll do fine," Robbie says. "Trust me."

"This is all sort of. Not what we had in mind, is it?"

"What do you think we had in mind?"

"Something, I don't know. Bigger? A vegetable garden. Kids and old people and animals. Chickens and goats and a friendly horse that keeps wandering off and the neighbor keeps bringing her home again."

"That's specific."

"I really think we should give Wolfe a house in the country," she says. "He deserves it. He's going to spend his life healing sick children."

"Yeah, maybe we should."

"For some reason I keep thinking about Columbus standing at the prow of his ship wearing a tiara."

"The magician hoves into view."

"What do you think it would have been like," she says. "Setting sight on a whole new continent, when you got up one morning and went on deck expecting to just see more and more ocean."

"We do remember that he was a mass murderer. The ships were financed by the Inquisition."

"Thanks, Professor. Okay, what would it be like to see a whole new continent, like that."

"It'd be a large experience. No denying."

"I mean, the *possibility* of it."

"Yeah," he says. "It would have been huge."

Robbie considers himself in the mirror, wearing eye shadow. He says, "I can't tell if I look glamorous or pathetic."

"Glamorous. No question. I like it when men do only one thing. Business suit and three-inch heels. Or, in your case, a T-shirt and a regular-guy haircut and eye shadow."

"If I wore eye makeup to work, I'd lose my job."

"What if Wolfe started dressing more gender-ishly?"

"I'd never find pictures of him like that."

"Only for us, then. You and I would know he wears heels, or lipstick. His followers wouldn't have to know. You and I can picture him in a T-shirt, jeans, and heels."

"If you really want to."

"You're right, though," she says. "His patients would freak out."

"As people do. When a responsible man in a responsible position turns up in eye shadow."

Long ago, when Isabel was seven or eight, when Robbie was four or five, she dressed him in a silk slip and their mother's pearls and marched him proudly downstairs, into the midst of a dinner party, which, as it turned out, was a gathering of people with powers potent enough to have inspired, earlier that day, an argument about whether to mention Jesse Jackson, or Israel. Robbie considered himself transmuted, his splendor fully revealed, as he walked a few paces ahead of his sister, into the dining room, in a waft of their mother's Shalimar. He's asked himself sometimes if it might have made a difference had their mother and father, their mother *or* their father, reacted differently. Robbie doesn't blame them. He's expended a good deal of effort not blaming them, though he does think— can't help thinking—that an invisible line runs from that night to the night, years later, when he told their parents he was turning down the offers from medical schools. He'd decided he didn't want to be a doctor after all. He'd seen on their father's face an expression like the one with which he'd greeted Robbie's entrance into the dining room, in pearls and perfume.

Robbie says to Isabel, "As RuPaul reminds us, you're born naked, and all the rest of it is drag. I'm not sure if Ru was thinking about pediatricians, though."

"But Wolfe can still get a house in the country, don't you think?"

"If you really want him to."

"His dog would love it, all that space to run around in."

"Arlette," he says. "The dog's name is Arlette. What about Lyla?"

"I think she'd come up for weekends, on the train," she says.

"Wouldn't he get lonely, though?"

"He'd have his practice. Office in town, all the local kids."

"Still."

"Okay . . . he'd meet a farmer."

"A single, gay farmer—"

"Who took over the family farm when his father died unexpectedly—"

"He killed himself?" Robbie asks.

"No. Tractor accident, something like that. So this guy came back—"

"From San Francisco . . . No, more like Maine."

"And he's been living on the farm in this kind of monkish renouncement. Up at five in the morning, bed by nine."

"He's older than Wolfe. Not *old* old. Fortyish. And he's not exactly handsome."

"Why not?" Isabel says.

"It'd be too . . . porn. Some Tom of Finland guy who happens to be a farmer."

"He's not ugly, though."

"No. He's regular. He's a regular-looking guy."

"If that's how you want him."

"Wait a minute. Are you *angry* about this?"

"No. You're right. The farmer should be regular attractive. He's more interesting that way."

"But you'd rather he was some kind of perfect specimen," he says.

She brushes on another hint of eye shadow. Is it too much? Robbie knows—it seems no one else does—that Isabel has never been quite sure about what she looks like. She's sometimes only semi-identifiable to herself, in photographs. She has, since childhood, been trying to catch glimpses of her authentic, immutable self.

She says, "I've always been a sucker for beauty. I guess you'd have to say that hasn't really proven to have been such a great idea—"

They are not, as far as Robbie is concerned, going to talk about her marriage, not this early in the morning. Isabel's cataloging of her own misjudgments will have to wait, at least until Robbie's had his second cup of coffee.

He says, "I'm going to go check on Dan and the kids."

"I'll be ready in, like, four minutes. I think the farmer reads Tolstoy for an hour every night, before he goes to bed."

"Or George Eliot. I kind of want him reading *Mill on the Floss.*"

"Okay, sure," she says. "And one day he runs into Wolfe, in town."

"They're both attracted to each other."

"Maybe they get to be best friends before one of them confesses—"

"The farmer confesses, first," he says.

"Do you want him to?"

"It's a bigger thing for him. He doesn't know any other gay people. And he's sure Wolfe will back away. But the farmer can't help himself. He has no idea Wolfe's been doing the same thing—"

"Holding back."

"Because Wolfe can't believe the *farmer* is interested. They've been like spies who didn't realize they were working for the same country."

"This sounds like something we could pitch to Netflix," she says.

"Yeah, maybe."

"It all seems perfect, at first. But then Wolfe's practice gets more and more demanding, and the farmer's homophobic grandmother has to move in with them."

"Do we need to get quite this *real*?"

"There has to be conflict," she says. "If we're going to pitch it to TV."

"Let's not pitch it to TV, okay?"

"Sorry. It's just that selling a TV show would take care of the whole money thing."

"Let's hold off on that, for now. Let's think about what'd be nice for Wolfe."

"What about Lyla?"

"What about her?"

"She's suddenly sort of . . . left out, isn't she?"

"Are you worried about her?" he says.

"Not at all. I just want Wolfe to be happy. Lyla can manage on her own."

"Plus, Lyla doesn't exist."

"Right. Of course she doesn't."

V iolet and Nathan sit at the kitchen table, awaiting the breakfast Dan is making for them. Nathan's thumbs fly at hummingbird speed over the keys of his phone. Violet sits up straight, hands folded on the tabletop, a posture she considers regal.

When Robbie walks in, he's already been stripped of his celebrity status. He got his flourish of greetings when he appeared in the children's bedroom. Now he's merely another adult.

Dan asks, "How you doing?"

It is, as Robbie can't help noticing, the second time this morning Dan has posed the question.

"Fine. I'm fine."

Violet says, "We're ready."

She's been rushed here in a skirt that, while appropriate, has robbed her of her own sense of enchantment—now she must walk, diminished, into the trials of the day. How is it possible that she's been called to breakfast earlier than necessary?

"Hang on," Dan says. He scrapes scrambled eggs out of the pan, onto two plates.

Dan is neither tragic nor melancholy. He's the harried servant of his children. He awaits his own comeback, but until then it's Dan the Knight Templar, finding dignity in service, willing to relinquish all appearances of power in the name of duty.

Does anyone miss the drugged-out Dan who took what he'd considered, at the time, to be a year or two off, when Nathan was born? Does anyone (other than Dan himself) mourn the dissolution of the stoned rocker, sweating, shirtless—the guy Dan had expected, years ago, to turn into again, effortlessly, after he gave up his music for a year, maybe two, to be home with his newborn son?

Dan scrapes butter across slices of whole-grain toast, and delivers the plates to the kids. Robbie refrains from reminding Dan that the doctor said Violet shouldn't have butter, or eggs for that matter, anymore. But hey, a little butter on a piece of toast . . .

Never mind about Dan allowing Robbie to be the fat-and-salt police. Robbie will talk to Dan about it, but not now, not this morning.

Violet regards her breakfast with patrician reluctance. Nathan continues tapping at his phone.

"Eat," Dan says.

Breakfast administered, Dan turns to Robbie. Dan's face is avid and ruddy, robust. Dan resembles himself, occupies himself, more effectively than anyone Robbie could name.

"I'm looking at another apartment today," Robbie says. "River view. Or so they claim."

"It's shocking, what things cost."

"Yeah, and when it's just me—"

Shit. Retract. Robbie's determination to be neither homeless nor heartbroken lapses every now and then, despite his best efforts.

Dan asks, "Are you still bummed about Oliver?"

"No. Fuck Oliver."

He glances at Violet, who either has not heard him say "fuck" or has heard it often enough already, by the age of five, to consider it a usual, everyday word. There's no house policy about swearing in front of the children. There is, for that matter, no house policy about almost anything.

"Which means it's time for you to start dating again, right?" Dan says.

It is, in fact, time to start dating again. But Dan has no idea what that means for a gay man well into his thirties who has neither money nor abs. Dan lives on the straight planet, where a thirty-seven-year-old guy who's single, presentable, and capable of sustained interest in another person is considered a prize. On Planet Gay, the conditions are less forgiving.

Dan says, "Back on the horse, man. Somebody's out there right now, looking for you. Coffee?"

"Sure."

Nathan says, "These eggs look weird."

Dan says, "You look weird."

"That hurts my feelings."

"Come on."

Violet says, "The eggs *are* funny."

"This is exactly the way I make them, every morning."

"They're kind of weird this morning," Nathan says. "There are these lumps."

Dan passes Robbie a coffee mug printed with the black-and-white image of Mount Rushmore. Dan says to the children, "Eat. The eggs. Please."

He's perfected a tone. He lowers his voice another half octave, betrays no impatience, but puts equal emphasis on every word, which means that negotiations have come to an end.

The household may lack rules and policies but Dan has developed, on his own, a manner of speaking that means, *This conversation is over.* Robbie wonders if the kids worry about Dan's wrath or if they worry about revoking his idea of himself as a benevolent but evenhanded father; someone who must, occasionally at least, be obeyed. What would they do if nobody possessed any powers of command or control?

Dan grins at Robbie, does a bit of an eye roll. *Kids. What can you do?* Dan says, "I finished the new one last night. Can I play it for you, later this morning?"

"You know you can."

"It's still pretty rough."

"I like it rough."

"I know you do."

Robbie can't recall when, exactly, he and Dan started up these erotic enactments of the ongoing flirtation that manifests itself as an admixture of frat brothers and long-married couple. These volleys of gay-speak are strictly private—they never occur when Isabel is in the room.

Dan knows—does he know?—that Isabel is already preparing for her departure. Maybe it's only Robbie who knows about it, this soon. Isabel herself may not know, yet.

Robbie comprehends Isabel's meaning when she talks about wanting something bigger. Robbie is fluent in Isabel's inner language. Something *else.* Something less *usual.* Something commensurate with her own capacity to want that which hovers at the far end of the visible range. A chaos of affection and good-natured argument. A friendlier, more rowdy domesticity. The lamp in the window, stars windblown among the trees.

Violet spills her juice. The juice gets onto Nathan's pants, which means Violet spilled it on purpose, which means Nathan blames Violet for everything, which means . . .

Dan attends to it. The spill vanishes at the stroke of a sponge, Nathan's pants are declared unblemished, accidents happen, we've got to *roll* with this, the world *awaits us*.

While Dan is occupied with the children, Robbie hits Google, *farm houses new york state,* finds a good one, downloads it, and shoots off a second post.

Image: A farmhouse, its clapboard turned by weather from white to ivory, chapel-like with its steeply peaked central gable, covered porches on either side shading spectral wicker chairs, the variegated off-whiteness afloat among spines of granite hills touched, here and there, by outcroppings of trees.

Caption: Just saw this house for sale. What if we were to buy it? Take the plunge.

Robbie posts it before he notices, a nanosecond too late, that in the photograph the leaves on the distant trees are going yellow with the first encroachment of fall.

Oops. This is supposed to be a picture from today, early April.

Immediately, it garners nine Likes.

No one seems to notice, or care, that the photo can't have been taken in April.

Dan pours Violet a new glass of juice. Nathan eyes her murderously. She is sucking the life force out of the kitchen and into herself, she is stealing from him, she's a thief and a tattle-tale and there's something creepy about her neck. Dan has re-trieved his coffee mug from the countertop, is partway through saying to Robbie, "I have a feeling..." when Isabel hurries into the room.

"Good morning," she says.

Violet jumps up and runs to her. Nathan remains sullenly seated.

"Good morning," Violet says eagerly. Ever since Violet began disliking her mother a year or so ago, she has been more extravagant in her demonstrations of affection.

Does she believe she can summon her mother back again—the engaged and attentive mother, it hasn't been all that long—by the force of her own vehement joyfulness? Why wouldn't she believe that?

Nathan deepens his voice as best he can, says, "Hey, Mom." *I'm the one who gets it about you, remember? I don't need to fawn over you. I'm your date for the long haul.*

Robbie and Dan are just two guys with coffee mugs, stand-ing in the vicinity of the refrigerator.

Isabel says, "Violet, do you think the hamster will have her babies today?"

"I think she had them already, when we weren't there."

"A girl does need her privacy sometimes. Nathan, are you going to be nice to Samantha?"

"She's *gross.*"

"But try not to break her heart, okay? You don't need to humiliate her."

Nathan shrugs. No promises.

"You can't blame her for being in love," Isabel says. "Hey, I have to go."

Dan says, "There's coffee."

"I've already ordered a Starbucks, on my way to the train. I am *insanely* late."

Isabel, for all her wandering attention, is still good at this: the mother who knows which questions to ask (the pregnant hamster, poor besotted Samantha) and which to avoid (Violet's difficulty with other girls her age, Nathan's grades). The mother who has to rush off because people are expecting her, because nothing can start without her.

How has Isabel learned to be this person, even if it's only for the sake of the kids? How did Dan master that voice? They've always been improvising, all three of the adults, and as Nathan and Violet have grown older they seem to have willingly accepted the fact that they are neither more nor less than the youngest members of a haphazardly formed crew that goes by the name "family" for obscure legal reasons. It's a shock, then, to be standing here, seeing (how has Robbie missed it?) that a *family* is exactly what these people have become, more or less involuntarily—a conglomerate of sorts that will survive its own ruptures, even the divorce Robbie sees coming, just as it will survive without him, living upstairs. The loss of a beloved uncle may be heartbreaking but the world, its geography and its weather, goes on. As Isabel hurries away, her hair semi-tamed into a semi-messy knot, her white blouse unbuttoned to the buttonhole that separates dignity from display, Robbie checks his Instagram. Wolfe's post about the country house, beamed in from the wrong season, has another twelve Likes.

After Isabel has gone, after the children have returned to their breakfasts, Robbie and Dan stand together, sipping their coffees.

"Here's to a place with a river view," Dan says. He and Robbie toast each other with their coffee mugs. Dan has the mug with the picture of Bob Dylan, obscenely young, from *Highway 61 Revisited*.

"Here's hoping this'll be the one," he adds.

His eyes, those Nordic baby blues, are innocent of depths. Dan, this Dan, has acquired an aura of cordial bafflement, as if he's unsure about what's happening but figures that it will, must, prove to be all right. The trouble with recovering addicts—with the in-house recovering addict—is this insistence on dividing his life into the addicted past, a country of secrecy and humiliation, and the clean, sober present, where he buys tulips on his way home from grocery shopping, where he's writing music again. A present in which everything conspires toward benediction, if only because it's not the past.

"Here's hoping," Robbie says.

Dan says, "Shouldn't you be off to work by now?"

"It's asbestos day. Remember?"

It seems lately that Dan needs more than one reminder about the ongoing facts of Robbie's life.

"Right," Dan says. "So, I can play you that song, this morning."

"Can't wait."

Dan knows. *Right, Robbie, you can't wait.* People think he doesn't know. He allows them to think that. If he is loved, in part, for some sort of circus-bear cluelessness, it's all right with him.

And really, if he comes off as sweetly delusional about his prospects, if Robbie and Isabel are humoring him, that's all right, too. Dan keeps his reasonable expectations to himself.

What neither Isabel nor Robbie knows: if you're delivering a song, there are instances when the veil of the ordinary falls away and you are, fleetingly, a supernatural being, with music rampaging through you and soaring out into a crowd. You connect, you're giving it, you're the living sweat-slicked manifestation of music itself, the crowd feels it as piercingly as you do. Always, almost always, you spot a girl. She doesn't need to be pretty. She's the love of *somebody's* life (you hope she is), and for those few seconds she's the love of yours, you're singing to her and she's singing back to you, by raising her arms over her head and swinging her hips, adoring you or, rather, adoring some being who is you and the song combined, able to touch her everywhere. It's the briefest of love affairs, sometimes consummated (sorry, Isabel), but whenever that happened, whenever Dan got lucky, he found that the affair had reached its climax when Dan hit a high C and held it and sent it spiraling out to her—how could anything fleshly, after that, fail to be at least slightly disheartening?

It didn't matter if those ecstatic connections occurred in some skanky club, or in even lesser places (Dan has played the bar in a Mexican restaurant in Cleveland). You didn't need Madison Square Garden to have it, the pure glory that showed itself only on occasion but was nevertheless an almost holy spasm, a wrenchingly public giving and losing of yourself, and yes, it could happen in a Mexican restaurant in Ohio and no, hardly anyone else has felt it, ever.

What Robbie and Isabel can't apprehend: Dan wants another of those moments, maybe two or three. He wants only that. He's singing ballads now, the rockier numbers no longer reside in him, but he can call forth the magic just as surely with protestations of beauty if they're deep and fierce enough. Consider Joni Mitchell, consider Neil Young. Dan can rock a room with these songs too, he can get under the skin of others, he can summon forth the glimmer of their living ghosts. That's all he wants. A little more of that. A little more of it. It's all he wants.

He says to Robbie, "Got to get Nathan off to school."

"You want me to take him?"

"No, you hang out with Violet, okay?"

"More than glad."

Violet's kindergarten has been cut back, temporarily, to afternoons only, as they search for someone to replace Gretta, who'd seemed fine until the day before yesterday, when she told the children to continue working on their construction-paper Easter eggs, walked out of the classroom, and vanished.

It can seem sometimes that the true end of civilization is starting not at the top, not among deluded politicians and corporate lords, not among polluters and terrorists, but at the bottom, among those who care for children, the people who can't be sure that the walls have been checked for toxicity or that no one will walk into a classroom in homemade camouflage and a Halloween mask, carrying a semiautomatic.

"Nathan," Dan says, "let's get you ready."

Robbie says, "Violet, it's you and me for a while."

Violet flings her arms over her head, shouts, "Hooray-dee-ay." Robbie is beginning to detect a note of falseness in her. Can she really be this happy about spending an hour alone with Robbie, who she sees every day? At what age do children begin to realize that they're expected, sometimes, to be parodies of children?

Or is she, like Robbie, simply aware of a restiveness in the air, between Isabel and Dan? Does she hope that a little girl's rampant enthusiasms, voiced often enough, will drown out whatever low murmuring, ominous if unintelligible, she's begun hearing, sometimes from under the bed, sometimes from inside a wall.

A woman weeping on the subway is always a stranger. To others and, more likely than not, to herself. Isabel has seen those women. She's wondered how they've let things get that far.

She loves the subway. She loves its racketing twenty-four-hour night world, the other passengers who serve to remind you that you are not by any means a typical member of the human species, not when, squeezed in among the suited commuters, are a tattooed boy with a Yorkshire terrier peeking out of his backpack, an Orthodox woman flanked by twin sons in *payot,* and a man wearing a bow tie, reading *The Golden Bowl* with ostentatious dignity, like the shade of a professor doomed to ride the 4 train, reading late James, until God decrees that he's finally arrived at his stop. It's one of Isabel's favorite parts of the day, this cacophonous, crowded nowhere, clattering between home and work but belonging to neither, a world of the in-between where, for short interludes, she's only a citizen of the subway itself.

She can tell she's started weeping when the man standing beside her shifts himself as far away as the crowd will permit. She hadn't realized.

She's as discreet as she's able to be. She gropes in her bag for the mini-pack of Kleenex, can't find it. She can feel the man (steel-gray crew cut, shaving cut on his chin) straining away from her, as do others (an Indian man wearing a bright blue suit, the boy with the Yorkie), whether out of respect for Isabel's distress or nervousness about her sanity or both.

Isabel has done it. Most people have. You do your best to avoid being noticed by the delusional, who may very well be waiting to aim a rant at the first person who makes eye contact. She knows, too, that neither her impeccable makeup nor her handbag (she lied to Dan about what it cost, men had no idea how much a bag could matter) categorically disqualifies her from the ranks of the potentially threatening.

She's not sure why this is happening. It has to do with drift, the sense that the gravitational pull isn't holding as it once did, which has to do with Robbie moving out and with Dan's determination to resuscitate a career that never quite existed, which everyone knows but Dan. It has to do with her ever less successful attempts to impersonate a mother. Violet knows she's faking; how is it that only the five-year-old can see it?

And yet she is loved and looked after. Her husband gets up early to make breakfast for the kids.

She wanted this. She wanted the marriage. She wanted the kids. She wanted the place in Brooklyn, refused to worry overmuch about the mortgage payments.

She wanted the job, too. She was good at it. She strove. She outperformed others. The trick now, it seems, is to keep wanting it, the job as well as the marriage, motherhood, the stratospherically costly handbag. The trick is learning not to despise herself for her claustrophobia and disappointment.

It's unprofound. It's *white lady problems.*

Even now she doesn't look back and say to herself, *That was a mistake* or *What was I thinking?* She and her brother were both in love with her husband, which made sense—what if she'd married someone Robbie didn't like? She'd wanted children. She still wants them but maybe not all the time, not every morning and every night. She'd had no reason not to expect that her job would continue, unabated. She'd thought she'd keep assigning stories to the most brilliant photographers, visiting them in their studios, seeing what eccentricities they'd wrought on stories as *un*eccentric as "New York's Greatest Dive Bars" and "Billionaires' Apartments." She'd assumed she'd always be able to tell them, *Don't worry, the magazine will run these—they'll do what I tell them to.*

It all made sense. It all made sense at the time. It all made sense before the Internet muscled print journalism onto the Endangered list and kept on nudging it in the direction of Extinct. It made sense until she fell out of love with Dan (more erosion than romantic catastrophe, just the steady thud of dailiness), until the children ceased to be pliable and endlessly, uncomplicatedly affectionate. It made sense until it was time for Robbie to go and live on the far side of town. There'd been every reason to anticipate a bigger apartment, a *series* of bigger apartments, an urban variation on the Amish, building new wings and second stories as the marriages and births accrued, as Robbie fell finally into love, as Robbie and Oliver or someone else (someone smarter than Oliver, please, someone more capable of irony) had their own children and the children formed a posse like the girls in *Little Women,* more self-reliant, less frightening in their fragility and their needs.

It has, until recently, seemed reasonable for her to anticipate more, because there was more to be had. Now she's like the woman in the fairy tale who demands more wishes from the magic fish, more and more, until the fish grows weary of her and takes it all away.

She isn't sure when she ceased to be the central figure in her own story and became, instead, the greedy and embittered sister, her own shadowy twin, the one who's been given everything and yet keeps on grumbling, *Not enough*.

Still, she hadn't expected to be weeping on the subway.

She looks down. It's better to look down, to relieve others of the threat of eye contact. There are the tips of her shoes, which, to her relief, are not quite touching the cordovan loafers of the man with the crew cut, who's mortified at finding himself pinned more closely to her than he'd like to be but can't draw too much attention to himself by pushing through the crowd to get farther away from her.

As the train pulls into Twenty-third Street there's a light tap on Isabel's shoulder. It's a woman in her sixties, dyed black hair and aviator glasses, who has stood up and is offering Isabel her seat.

In a parallel world Isabel would take the woman's hands in hers and say, "Old Mother, I didn't recognize you at first." In a parallel world they'd console each other, share a wry laugh about it all, marvel at the fact that everybody isn't weeping on the subway all the time.

In this world, in this city, Isabel nods gratefully and accepts the vacated seat, works her way in between a scowling woman playing Candy Crush on her cell and an elderly man embracing a sack full of what appears to be dirty laundry.

Isabel is embarrassed about her sadness. She's embarrassed about being embarrassed about her sadness, she who has love and money. She tries looking discreetly into her bag for a Kleenex, without anything that could be called frantic rummaging. She ponders the prospect that decadent unhappiness might, in its way, be worse than genuine, legitimate despair. Which is, as she knows, a decadent question to pose at all.

After Dan and Nathan have been seen to the front door, amid a flurry of blown kisses and farewells from Violet, Violet says, "What should we do?"

"What do you *want* to do?"

"I don't know."

Before Violet and Nathan arrived, Robbie had not anticipated children's dearth of ideas about what to do next. It's surprisingly possible to worry about that with a child, and with Violet in particular, as if you're giving a party that's not going all that well.

"Want to build something with your blocks?" he says.

"Maybe."

"Or not."

"No, we could build something with my blocks—"

She appears to be struggling with a mitigating factor, something that renders the blocks fine, as toys go, but untenable for some reason.

Robbie says, "Let's go to your room and pick something out."

Violet, who is usually avid to go anywhere, even to her own room, remains with her feet (ballet slippers, Robbie hasn't brought up the subject of footwear yet) planted on the floorboards.

"When are you going?" she says.

"Now. To your room. With you."

"No, I mean, when are you going?"

Where has this question come from? Haven't Robbie, Dan, and Isabel agreed not to mention it to the kids until Robbie's settled on a new apartment, a place they can visit the day Robbie signs the lease? Neither Violet nor Nathan, after all, remembers a time when Robbie didn't live upstairs.

Violet must have overheard something. Try keeping secrets from children, whose very lives depend on listening, and knowing.

Violet, however, seems at times to know that which she could not possibly know. The day Robbie met Adam (*You look different today, Robbie*), the expensive shoes Robbie bought and, guiltily, returned (*I think you should have nicer things*).

As Isabel has put it, *God, I hope she isn't psychic.*

"I'm only going to your room," Robbie says. "Now. With you."

"But you'll come back."

"Sweetheart, if I ever go anywhere, I'll always come back."

She nods, unconvinced. Is it a mistake, to conceal from Violet and Nathan, however temporarily, the fact that Robbie is moving to another apartment? Will they feel betrayed when they learn that a secret has been kept from them? Again, always, the fundamental question: are you protecting your children or are you sowing the seeds of what will prove to be a lifetime of mistrust?

The intercom chimes. Violet says, "Who do you think it is?" Her tone is both alarmed and anticipatory.

Robbie says, "Let's find out. Hello?"

Tinged with the faintest undertone of static: "Hey, it's me."

"Who?"

"Chess. It's Chess."

Robbie, aware of Chess's irritation over his failure to imme-diately recognize *Hey, it's me,* buzzes her in. During the min-ute it takes her to mount the stairs (he can hear her boot clomps through the door), Robbie says to Violet, "Who do we think this is?"

"It's *Chess,*" Violet answers impatiently. Another recent de-velopment: the question of when Violet does, and when she does not, want to be treated as a child younger than she actu-ally is.

Then Chess, holding Odin, is at the door.

"Hey, Chess," Robbie offers. Here she is. Here is her magni-tude and her buzz cut, her swarm of tattoos. Here she is at just past nine in the morning, holding Odin, who, five months old, mutters contentedly at her breast.

It seems, fleetingly, that the world is a stream of ever-younger children, that Nathan has already, at ten, been hur-ried offstage to make room for his replacement, and that the clock might be ticking for Violet, as well.

Violet shouts gleefully, "Hello Chess, hello Odin, good morning!"

"Good morning, gang," Chess says. Her soft, flutelike voice is incongruous, emanating as it does from a person of her bear-ing; from her broad, rosy face, with its deep-set eyes and small, firm mouth.

"Do you want some pancakes?" Violet says. It's unclear how she assumes that pancakes could suddenly be produced.

"Thanks," Chess says. "I'm okay." To Robbie she adds, "Sorry to drop by like this. I tried calling."

Robbie passes through a twinge of guilt. Shouldn't adults caring for children keep their phones on, all the time?

He says, "Let me guess."

"Is Dan here?"

"Back in a bit. Come in."

"I can't stay."

"I know." Robbie extends his arms for Odin. Chess hands him the baby, carefully, gratefully. Robbie is astonished, still, by this warm, compact parcel of life. He knows Odin is also a fussy creature with a cohort of panicky and sometimes incomprehensible needs. And yet, in taking Odin, this placid Odin, from Chess there's a passing of the torch that, in some other civilization, might be perpetuated by adults who simply keep passing a baby among themselves, for the warmth and hope it implies.

Chess, relieved of Odin, steps deeper into the foyer. It would be too rude, no matter what the clock says, to simply dump Odin like a bag of groceries and move along.

"I've got coffee," Robbie says. "Pancakes would be more challenging."

"I'm already late. I promise I won't keep doing this."

"We don't mind."

"Garth and I are going to have a conversation," she says.

Robbie nods. No denying the need for a conversation with Garth.

"I should be back by three," Chess says. "It's only the one class today, plus office hours."

"No rush."

"Thanks. Bye, Violet."

"Bye-bye, Chess." Violet blows Chess an extravagant, parade-float kiss.

After Chess has gone, her boot thumps diminishing down the stairs, Violet says, "I've got toys for Odin."

"Great. Why don't you go get them?"

"I'll be *right back*."

"Great."

Yet another new one: Violet's underlying worry that if she's absent from any room, any event, for too long, the world will forget about her.

How is it possible that a five-year-old girl is already developing a hint of mortal wistfulness, the nascent fear of her own disappearance?

Robbie looks into Odin's face. Odin looks back, searchingly. He regards Robbie less with mute perplexity than with curiosity and hesitant recognition, as if he's seen Robbie before, somewhere, but can't remember where.

The sidewalk in front of the school is crowded with children and parents. Dan doesn't mind, he's determined not to mind, that for the last two blocks Nathan has been walking several paces ahead of him.

It was bound to happen. Dan simply wasn't expecting it quite so soon. Nathan has already developed a different walk, more stride to it, more assurance. He marches forward, backpack slung over his left shoulder, in his hoodie and jeans and his silver Nikes.

This is right. This is as it should be. It's just that it's happening so soon.

Ahead: the pearly limestone of the school itself, its stolid Beaux Arts dignity, its arches and colonnades.

Ahead, as well: Chad and Harrison, Nathan's posse, waiting for him with their recently acquired loutish indifference. It's boy world now, affections implied but no longer demonstrated. Chad and Harrison are waiting for Nathan. It's sufficient proof of their affection.

Dan would prefer to be happier about Chad and Harrison, who, at the age of ten, are able somehow to look as if they've been passing a cigarette back and forth after they were dropped off by their mothers, who are friendly to each other but only cordial to Dan: the mothers who work in an unspecific way *in finance;* who belong to the cohort of New Yorkers who might as well be Dutch burghers from the nineteenth century; who are not charmed by Dan's hair or his Ramones T-shirt, which, apparently, speaks to them not of boho insouciance but of middle-aged desperation.

At least this morning they've already dumped their boys at school and hurried off. At least they'll all be spared any attempts at conversation. Relations with the parents of your kids' friends can be like those of rival dukes and duchesses, forced into civility solely because you belong to the same ruling house.

Chad and Harrison wear their own tight jeans and hoodies, their own silver shoes. Nathan quickens his pace, eager to reach them, bulling his way among the other kids, who, for the most part, still resemble children: the two shrieking girls dressed in pink, the red-haired boy who carries, with exquisite caution, a goldfish in a glass bowl as his mother—who has the decency to be untidy, to be wearing a man's tweed overcoat—exhorts her son to be even more careful with the goldfish bowl, to please remember that bringing it to school with him is a big responsibility and was not her idea in the first place.

Chad and Harrison ignore the others, the noisy girls and the boy bearing the fish. They nod in Nathan's direction. Dan would prefer not to notice that Chad and Harrison are, essentially, a twosome, with Nathan as their third; that Chad and Harrison have come earlier into the first intimations of minuscule manhood; that Nathan imitates them in ways they do not imitate him. Nathan lacks Chad and Harrison's wised-up, taciturn knowingness, their early attempts at tough-guy slouches. Nathan is kinder than his friends, less precociously cynical, which is good, a good thing about him for the long run, even if it's going to hamper him now, although for Nathan *now* is all that matters.

Dan knows, too, that Nathan's stock has fallen because he's

suddenly, persistently adored by a girl named Samantha, a peripheral figure, homely and solitary, whose affections for Nathan indict Nathan himself. If he emitted a stronger force field,
a girl like this would never dare. She reduces him, just by being
smitten.

Dan says, "See you later, buddy."

"See you later," Nathan mutters.

Dan would like to ask him, *Do you have any idea?* Do you
think, even fleetingly, about how much has been done for you,
along with the birth gifts themselves: white and healthy and
smart. Pure luck. Do you get it that .00001 percent of ten-year-
old boys get any of this, never mind all of it?

Dan would never ask those questions. It's an accomplish-
ment of sorts that Nathan sails through it all unencumbered by
gratitude or guilt. It's part of what a parent can give a child.
Dan hopes, he can only hope, that that's true. He cherishes the
prospect that Nathan will someday see the bigger picture, once
he's less occupied with being a member of it, which is, for Nathan, a full-time occupation, one at which he's only barely suc-
ceeding. He is more encumbered by his father than he is by his
fortune or his failures. And once his father has set him free,
he's off to be with his boys, to embark for another day on his
journey away from his life of shame and chagrin, from his
sense of his own indenturehood, from childhood itself, away
from all of it, away.

R obbie holds Odin on the sofa with Violet pushed up close, whispering, "Hey, Odin, hi, this is Violet, I love you."

Pressing Odin between his upper arms, Robbie manages, awkwardly, to send out Wolfe's third post on his iPad:

Image: A white porcelain coffee cup steaming on a kitchen tabletop alongside Arlette's chewed-up red leash, dangling its brass hook over the table's edge, where, just out of range, Arlette would be staring at the leash's suspended end, whimpering with anticipation.

Wolfe and Lyla's apartment is an amalgam of three places: the loft in which the dog lives (MommaGirl-Bronx), a stylishly scabrous apartment with rippled tin ceilings and scraps of ancient wallpaper still clinging to its walls (MattPhotoGuy), and a place somewhere in the East Village, meticulously furnished in mid-century modern (Bibi&Julie). Robbie has chosen them so judiciously that they look like different rooms in the same apartment.

Caption: Time for Arlette to go chase the pigeons!

Robbie sends it out. And a moment later . . .

Oops, Wolfe is upstate with Lyla today. Driving through a fall landscape that miraculously exists in April.

Robbie isn't usually this careless. Blame it on Christopher Columbus. Blame it on an as-yet-unseen apartment that will almost certainly be dim and stale-smelling or divided into sur-really tiny rooms or imbued with the continual sound of car horns and radios or all of the above, along with the river view, which will prove to be a sliver of the Hudson you can see from the kitchen window if you stand on a stool . . .

. . . the as-yet-unseen apartment that's at least an hour away from here but that Robbie may rent anyway, if it's passable, because he's starting to worry that his apartment hunt is becoming absurd. He's seen more than a dozen and even if Isabel and Dan are sorry about the move, they must—how could they not—be starting to entertain doubts. Is Robbie exaggerating the drear and squalor of what a sixth-grade teacher can afford? Is he delaying his own departure by reporting back on domestic prospects that can't, surely, be quite *that* bad?

Wolfe's post—the coffee cup on the kitchen table, even with its out-of-sequence incongruity—elicits sixteen Likes. People assume Wolfe's posts aren't always strictly chronological. Instagram exists, after all, outside the time-space continuum. It can be *Time to go chase the pigeons!* just as, simultaneously, it's time to drive through Vermont (or New Hampshire) thinking about buying a country house beamed in from another season and another time.

sabel should be in the office. She's on her way. She's merely taking some extra time getting there from Grand Central.

Until this morning, she's never walked unhastily through the Grand Central concourse. She's always been in a rush—to get to work, to get home again—and she realizes, as she walks slowly among the other travelers, that with the exception of student backpackers and baffled tourists, you are expected by Grand Central to be passing through on your way to urgent business elsewhere.

You are not encouraged to linger. There are no benches. There is no waiting room. Grand Central implies, with its august enormity and its unaccountable hush (people are, Isabel supposes, too rushed to make noise), that there is only motion, that your destination may promise rest and respite but here, in this monument to transit, you'd better keep moving.

Isabel pauses below the departures board.

9:45   Dobbs Ferry
10:01   Manitou
10:11   Cold Spring

What if she were the kind of person who could get on a train bound for an unfamiliar destination, who could vanish like the mythical man who goes out for a pack of cigarettes and is never heard from again? She considers what it would be like to be able to abandon all her gifts, all that's been lavished upon her; to be that careless and callous; to abandon everyone and get on a train. Someone who could shed a life as if it were an old coat, who could find her way to another life without having to suffer the recriminations: subject to a form of reincarnation, the kind that allows people (some, there must be some such people) to rent an apartment in a small town on the Hudson, to become a waitress in a diner, wearing a nametag that bears the name you've given yourself. Pearl, or Jasmine, or Naomi.

Dan, back at home, sits on the sofa, playing his new song for Robbie. Robbie, holding Odin on his lap, does his best to listen. But Odin is in pre-squall, the attentive, tremblingly aware condition that precedes a fit of crying, as if he senses some menace not apparent to anyone else in the room. Violet, having tired of Odin's refusal to be seduced by her or by the three dolls (including the upsetting ultrarealistic baby doll everyone is eager for Violet to outgrow), the googly-eyed stuffed frog, or the paper-flower garland, squats on the floor, studiously building a tower of the old-fashioned wooden blocks Robbie bought for her last week.

It's difficult to know which gifts Violet will like and which she'll politely accept and put away in her room, never to be touched again. Robbie has begun favoring toys that aren't so stubbornly girly. He doesn't want to keep giving her feather wings and ballerina dresses, though he knows she'd be happy to keep receiving them, no matter how many she's already got. Robbie has decided, instead, on the hit-or-miss. Squeakee the Balloon Dog and the Lego castle kit were failures. This set of old-fashioned blocks, however, appears to be an instant classic. How can the desires of another person, even at the age of five, be so opaque and unpredictable?

Dan finishes the song, which Robbie has, for the most part, failed to hear. He's been waiting for Odin to launch into that imminent fit of pique, for Violet's tower of blocks to come tumbling down.

Dan looks expectantly at Robbie. For a moment it's easy to see Dan when he was a boy, nervously hoping for praise, anticipating otherwise. Robbie knows, all too well, about Dan's mother's parsimony toward her sons and their accomplishments.

"Lovely," Robbie says.

"Too lovely?"

"No. It's emotional. True feeling isn't *too lovely*."

Robbie bounces Odin on one knee. Odin murmurs with pleasure. The fit has been forestalled, for now.

"I think maybe it's too sentimental," Dan says.

Dan's mother inspired in him a hunger for criticism. It's the only reaction he can trust. How did Garth, then, only three years younger, grow up to be so convinced that all criticism is either ignorance on the part of others or flattery in disguise? Did the two of them silently agree to split the damage?

Robbie says, "Maybe think about the garden thing." There were, he thinks, a couple of lines about a woman as a garden.

"I knew it. It's a cliché, right?"

"Not exactly. Maybe more like a little abstract. Maybe stay with the woman herself, not compare her to anything."

Dan produces a scrap of a smile, having received the required element of mild reprimand.

"There's a reason I always play everything for you first," he says.

Is Robbie essentially a more user-friendly incarnation of Dan's mother? Probably. Does he mind? Hard to say.

Violet says, "Look how tall my tower is getting."

"You go," Robbie tells her.

"It might fall down."

"That's the chance you take when you're dreaming big."

"I am. Dreaming big."

"That's good."

"But I really don't want it to fall down."

"If it does, you can build it again."

He can tell by her clouded expression that this was the wrong answer. What, however, would the right answer have been?

Dan says, "What about 'trance' and 'abundance'?"

"What about them?"

"Does it seem forced?"

Odin gets restless again. Being bounced on Robbie's knee has turned from delight to vexation. Robbie lifts him to his chest, holds him close, but that's not what Odin wants, either.

"Hey, buddy," Robbie whispers. "Are you getting tired? Think it's time for a nap?"

Dan says, "I like 'abundance.' I think 'trance' is really mostly there to semi-rhyme with 'abundance.'"

"Maybe you don't need to rhyme at all."

"Yeah, but I want two words that sound like twins, separated at birth."

"I can't believe you just said that."

Dan says, "What about 'took our chance' instead of 'in our trance'?"

"Try it."

Dan starts the song again. Odin mewls, fussily, into Robbie's chest. Violet puts another block onto the top of her tower, says, "I *really* hope it doesn't fall down." The floor is littered with toys. The baby doll lies facedown, an unsettlingly real simulation of infant mortality.

Violet says, "I hope hope hope it doesn't fall down," in a singsong voice, as Dan starts up on the song, again. They could be performing a duet. This time, Robbie listens attentively as Dan sings.

We thought we were immortal lovers,
We'd read our Byron and our Keats . . .

It's familiar—how many men have sung laments about lost love—but what's wrong with that? It's gutsy of Dan to assume that his as-yet-nonexistent listeners will know who Byron and Keats are, or won't mind that they don't.

Will those potential listeners be eager to hear ballads by a forty-year-old father with thinning, bleached-blond hair?

You don't ask that question. Dan needs his discouragement in reasonable doses. He needs his deeper optimism to remain intact. He's not naïve about the challenges, the thwartments and doubts, but he maintains that his efforts are subject to remedy through hard, persistent work. Dan, who scoffs at religion, doesn't know how deeply his Protestant lineage resides in him. A Dan who'd been raised Catholic, like Robbie and Isabel, would wait prayerfully for enlightenment. This Dan simply starts the song over. "Chance" instead of "trance."

He finishes singing the next couplet, *We thought that endings were for others . . .*

Good, don't strain for the rhyme . . .

. . . We were beauty, not the beast . . .

Not sure about that . . .

As Dan is about to start the next couplet Garth slams open the front door. On the word "beast." He stands glowering in the doorway, as if he's caught Dan and Robbie in an act of collusion.

There's no getting around Garth's cockeyed good looks. His narrow, sculpted face, his straggles of dirty-blond hair, his sinewy, agitated body.

Finally, Odin starts bawling, and Violet's block tower falls. Which sets Violet crying, as well.

Only Dan remains calm. He says, "Hey there," to Garth.

Garth steps inside. He says, "I was, like, five minutes late."

"In parent time, five minutes can be long."

"Hey, Garth," Robbie says.

Garth retracts Scary Guy. It's a talent, of sorts. That said, the rawer Garth, the beast, may get him killed one day. Garth, when he's being aggressive, is the kind of person who gets cut open in an argument in a bar, whose crazy neighbor finally shoots him for refusing to turn the music down. Robbie can only hope Garth is able to survive his life.

"Hey, Robbie," Garth says. "Sorry, guys. Thanks for being here."

"No problem," Dan tells him. "Here is where we are."

Violet ceases crying. It was only a hiccup of tears to begin with, a minor demonstration of her own misfortunes, lest they go unnoticed.

"What's the matter?" Garth says.

"My blocks fell down."

"Shit happens. Let's build them again."

"Okay."

Shouldn't a father, even a semi-father like Garth, attend first to his own wailing child? Does he think of Robbie as some sort of dependable, imperturbable nanny?

Garth kneels on the floor with Violet, lays down two of the larger blocks.

"We need a solid base," he says.

"Yes."

Robbie ponders, not for the first time, Violet's adoration of Garth. Maybe it's because Garth doesn't care much about her. Maybe there's more dignity for her, in that. Robbie rocks Odin, whose tears do not let up.

Robbie says, "I think our guy here could use a nap."

Garth, still kneeling with Violet and her blocks, reaches for Odin. Robbie passes through an impulse to refuse to relinquish the child. He settles for saying, "Be careful," as he hands Odin, a noisy bundle, to Garth.

"I'll do my best," Garth says. He takes Odin in his arms, says, "Hey there, guy, you're good, you're fine, all's well here."

Odin, emitting the breathy ends of his unhappiness, settles into the crook of Garth's arm. Garth, with his free hand, lays another block beside the first two.

"Odin is happy you're here," Violet says.

"Glad somebody is. I think we need four blocks for the base. What do you think?"

"I think so too."

How is it that Garth—feckless and irresponsible, narcissistic—can work this kind of magic? What's wrong with people? Babies, even. What's wrong with babies?

Dan says, "Chess isn't happy."

"How would you feel about getting off my back?"

"I'll think about it."

Dan and Garth. Survivors of their parents' lifeless marriage, of their mother's prim dignity and their father's desire to seek less dignity elsewhere.

Violet says, "This is a *very* good solid base."

"Okay," Garth says. "Let's start on the walls."

Dan says, "You're going to have to work this out with Chess."

"I thought you were thinking about getting off my back."

"I'm just stating the obvious."

"I will. Work things out. With Chess."

"We're always here if you need us," Robbie says. When did he become the house appeaser? When did he miss his chance to be volatile and delicate? He does possess those qualities. He hopes he does.

"Sweet of you," Garth answers. "But I'm kind of managing in my own half-assed way."

"I didn't mean—"

"Okay, mini-man and I are off to further adventures."

Violet says, "We have to finish the tower."

"Sorry, mamacita. You're in control. I'll check in with you later."

Dan says, "What if we all went to the park for a while?"

"Sure. Let's make it a party."

Robbie says, "I have to be at work soon. The asbestos crew promised to be done by noon."

"There's asbestos?" Garth asks.

"No. They have to make sure there's *not* asbestos, even though we all know there isn't."

Garth, who rarely requires more details than necessary, says, "Okay, then, it's a foursome."

Violet says, "We can visit the dogs in the dog run."

"We totally can."

"Dad, when are we getting *our* dog?"

"Soon," Dan tells her. "Soonish."

"A schnoodle."

"I know."

"I'll feed her and walk her every day."

"I know you will. Come on. Get your jacket."

"I don't want to wear my jacket."

"Get your jacket. It's chilly out."

"I'll be warm enough."

"Get your jacket. If you're too warm, you can take it off."

Violet stands obediently, goes to the closet for her jacket. It's easy to forget how ardently children like to be told what to do. Robbie would have said, *Fine, forget the jacket,* and would have pretended to agree with Violet when, once they got to the park, she insisted she wasn't cold.

Garth, holding Odin, says to Robbie, "Hey, a man with a job can't just go off to the park, right?"

"Right."

Robbie can only ask himself why he doesn't hate Garth more than he does. It's not easy, being Garth. It's not easy being anyone. But it can, at times, seem ever so slightly easier, being Garth, than it is being Robbie.

If you're Garth, you live in a rent-controlled apartment on East Tenth. You ride your Ducati to your studio in the Bronx and work on the fetishistic sculptures—scraps of wood, gesso and tar, each named after a Shakespeare play—that people, some people, admire but hardly anyone wants to buy. You're smarter than you appear to be, you who are all *bro* and *dude* in public but who's recently finished a totem made of creosote, mirror shards, and bear claws and called it *Cymbeline*. You get lucky, more often than not, on Tinder or in bars or just hanging out on a bench in the park. You don't worry about being no longer young. You know you've still got plenty of time. Whenever you're ready, there'll be an attractive if slightly weary woman who'll have run through her own body of adventures and be happy to sign on with you.

Robbie would be better able to hate Garth if he weren't at least a little bit in love with him. Or, more accurately, if he weren't in love with Garth's Garth-ness, his self-regard, his conviction that although his good intentions don't always please others, he is never, not truly, in the wrong. It's difficult for Robbie to separate being in love with Garth from a more insidious desire to *be* Garth, to be so unworried and unashamed.

Violet returns with her jacket, the faux Burberry Robbie bought for her. "Let's *go*," she says, as if she were the one who's been kept waiting.

"Let's totally go," Garth says.

Robbie sees them to the door. Violet says, "Do you think the Chihuahua will be there?"

"It might be," Dan says. "We can only wait and see."

She says to Robbie, "The Chihuahua is my favorite."

"I know."

"She's an—"

"Albino," Robbie says. "I know, I've seen him."

"I think she's a she."

"She probably is."

"Let's *go*," Violet says, and scurries out the door.

"Off to the park," Dan says.

"Off to the park with you."

"Thanks," he says.

"For what?"

"For listening to my song."

"I love listening to your songs."

"And for—"

A silence descends. Would Dan have liked to say, *Thanks for knowing that you really do have to move out? Thanks for being so good about our ability to manage on our own?*

No. Whatever Dan may have wanted to thank Robbie for, it wouldn't have been that. It would have been more like *Thanks for being my brother-friend,* which, concealed within, invisible to Dan himself, would be the more specific gratitude to Robbie for being someone who gets the picture—the extents and the limitations.

Robbie says, "I hope you find the Chihuahua."

Dan nods. "Yeah, hope we do."

He hesitates before leaning in and kissing Robbie on the lips. The hesitation is unusual, not the kiss. They've been kissing each other, quickly but tenderly, for years.

This time, however, Dan pauses, as if the kiss, this morning's kiss, is not quite, not exactly, the customary peck of endearment.

Not that there's anything erotic about it. There never is, never has been. Dan must have paused because, this morning, it's the home-style variation on a Judas kiss. It's Dan's way of telling Robbie, *I'll be sorry when you go.*

Robbie and Dan know they've become the central couple. Isabel is, increasingly, a dream they're having. They both know it. Robbie and Dan are the ones whose union is thriving, the ones who minister to each other, who are raising children together, who juggle the tasks, who want to know, each to the other, if they're *all right,* relatively speaking.

"Are you *coming?*" Violet calls from the hallway.

Robbie says to Dan, "I wish you whole flocks of albino Chihuahuas."

"You're the best," Dan replies. Then he and Garth, Odin, and Violet are off, in search of a white Chihuahua or, if that dog isn't there, in search of another to be Violet's new favorite. The apartment, with Robbie as its sole occupant, settles all but imperceptibly into its silent perpetuity, the quality that will be unaffected when these people are gone and others take their place. But for the moment Robbie is here, alone. Waiting for him upstairs are a dozen more essays on Christopher Columbus, which do have to have been read by the time the asbestos crew is finished.

t's *House of Mirth* today.

"Don't you think Lily has choices?" Chess asks Marta Grig, the sophomore who always claims the seat to Chess's immediate left, in defiance of the general agreement that no one at a seminar table sits within three or more seats of the professor.

Marta says, "Well, yes, she can choose between marrying someone she doesn't love and life as a spinster in some crappy apartment. That would fall under the general category heading of *Choice,* I suppose."

Marta, sea-blue hair, face pale and wistful as a mermaid's, smiles seductively at Chess. *Come on, disagree, I want you to.*

Chess says, "Don't you think by adding Selden into the mix, Wharton gives Lily a choice?" Chess notices that, on the blackboard, the words *ilver + mountain = epi* have been imperfectly erased by the room's previous professor.

"Outwardly, yes," Marta answers. "However. Lily wants to be a person of consequence. She wants to be *visible.* For that, she needs money. Do you think marrying Selden is really an option, for her?"

Marta is a nineteen-year-old who speaks in full sentences, who says "outwardly" and "however." She thinks she and Chess are an academic comedy team of sorts, one whose schtick is arguments delivered in elaborately courteous tones that only serve to emphasize their mutual disdain.

"You don't think Lily's weakness for fancy dresses affects her capacity to choose?" Chess says.

"You don't think fancy dresses are a symbol of power?"

"Of course they are. But she doesn't care about society. She despises most of those people. It's all about dresses and rose gardens, for her. She could have chosen love, instead."

Marta pauses. Isn't it sentimental, isn't it *cheap,* to suggest that love matters above everything? Isn't that the easy consolation of pulp fiction and B movies?

As Marta considers her counterattack, Chess continues: "I think Lily's real tragedy is her triviality. She's too easily convinced. She can't bear to miss parties she doesn't really want to go to. She wants things she doesn't really want. And so, she waits too long for love and money in the form of a man. And so, she loses her chance to marry Selden."

Marta, recovered, says, "She lives in a world where 'dingy' equals 'nobody.' If she married Selden, she'd be nobody. Do you think of that as a *choice,* for her?"

"She'd be somebody to him."

"But she'd be nobody to herself. How could she possibly be expected to choose that?"

You win this one, Marta. Lily Bart is a casualty of capitalism. The professor is cheap and sentimental.

What you don't know, Marta: outside the classroom the professor is a beleaguered mother, someone who may have been a bit hasty in her choice of a sperm donor. She is someone with a vaporizer and three copies of *Goodnight Moon* and a wardrobe of variously stained clothes she wears over and over, whenever she's not teaching.

"Did you read the Vivian Gornick?" Chess asks the class.

The ensuing silence implies that if any of them read it, they're reluctant to admit to it in front of others who haven't. They favor their outlaw reputations—why should one of them admit to having done the assigned reading if others have not?—over Chess's estimation of them.

But really, why should it be otherwise? Neither Chess nor Lily Bart can offer sex, intoxicants, access to clubs downtown, or the prospect of a lifelong friendship. Chess was once less tolerant of that than she is now. She seems to have shed a measure of her professorial sternness, her capacity for disapproval. She doesn't find that she misses them all that much.

She says, "Okay, we'll get back to Gornick. Let's say this. When Lily is required to give in, some flat, cold remove overtakes her. She's taken a long look at her own future, and it repels her. And suddenly, sentimental love becomes a thing of the past."

Chess is met with another shuffling silence. Class ends in less than twenty minutes. The students are already thinking about packing up.

Chess says, "Stefano, what do you think?" She generally prefers not to call on students who haven't volunteered. But she's angry and discouraged and there are, after all, twenty minutes still to go.

Stefano, who has been surreptitiously checking his phone (does he really suppose Chess can't tell?), says, "I think white people are fucked up."

Appreciative laughter ensues. Can't argue with that.

Chess says, "No question about it. We are, however, stuck, this week, with a novel about white people."

"I hope we're moving on soon," says Alanna, who usually prefers disapproving silence to delivering an opinion.

"We are. If you've read the syllabus."

Another bad move. The professor should never shame her students.

Marta steps in: "And yet, we should know about the white literary tradition, even if it's mostly horseshit."

In an alternate reality, where Chess and Marta are peers, they're merrily argumentative friends. They go for drinks together, bicker endlessly about literature and politics with the rousing, competitive respect of athletes on the same team.

Chess says, "What we're seeing here, in *House of Mirth,* is anti-Semitism and misogyny, but it's also more or less the end of the marriage story."

She has, at least, commanded a hiccup of attention from the class, however short-lived it may prove to be. Her students tend to be interested in the ends of things, particularly those that should not have existed in the first place.

She says, "Wharton doesn't know it, but Joyce is on the other side of the Atlantic, already working on *Ulysses.* Which will blow her right out of the water."

Alanna says, "Do you think of Wharton as *blown out of the water?*"

Another bad move on Chess's part. Wharton, standing suddenly beside Joyce—his smug disregard, his icy heart—has been forgiven her wealth, her prejudices, all her failings. Your mother may seem foolish and naïve until you hear your father's key in the front door.

"No," Chess says. "We seem to be reading Wharton this week. What I mean is, here come the modernists. Here come the writers who won't only rethink narrative without the marriage plot at its center, they'll convey women's freedoms *within* a marriage. Consider *Mrs. Dalloway.*"

Marta says, "I'm not sure how much freedom there is *within* anything."

Stefano adds, "The modernists were all rich white people, have I got that right?"

"They were," Chess says. "I wish they weren't."

She would like to lay her head down on the tabletop. She'd like to say, *Have mercy.* She'd like to say, *It used to seem like being a lesbian who's written about her South Dakota childhood, being brutalized by men, was enough.* She'd like to say, *I didn't think being old, what you think of as old, would matter this much.*

Her phone buzzes in her jeans pocket. It's Garth, to apologize. No one else has this number.

Eleven minutes more of class. Chess admits silently, to herself, that she'd rather argue with her students than talk to Garth about showing up late, yet again. At least her students will be gone at the end of the semester. And besides, Marta has more to say about the end of the marriage narrative. As well she should. Then it will be time for Chess to chastise them for failing to have read the Gornick essay, to lament (subtly) their general dearth of curiosity and (far more effective) imply that there just might be a quiz about Gornick's views at the start of the next class.

First, though, she needs to wind up the debate with Marta. What Chess won't say to her: *You might be shocked someday to learn how hard it is to dismantle the marriage narrative. You have no idea, not yet, how persistent that motherfucker can be.*

Although Robbie isn't packing up yet, he's begun sorting through the small stuff, that which has long resided behind a book on the bookshelf or at the bottom of a seldom-opened drawer. Robbie, veteran of numerous moves, has learned that before the moving-out process begins in earnest, before the sofa and tables and bed have been hauled onto a TaskRabbit's truck, an apartment, any apartment, however diminutive, still seems to be made up of uncountable, generally inconsequential, items that for most of their endless inanimate existences simply move from one place to another. They were acquired for valid reasons but have, for some time, existed strictly for the purpose of transit. They are held and examined only when they're about to be moved to their next location.

Among those objects are the easy, if relatively perplexing, ones: three boxes of paper clips, a half dozen blank notebooks, enough nails and screws to build an entire house. Although you don't need that many paper clips or notebooks, they are possessed of purpose, and can be packed without sensations of loss or regret. At least you'll never run out of paper clips (which does not mean you won't forget, and buy a fourth box of them a year or two from now); you can start jotting down more notes—ideas, dreams, details (the elderly man in the Batman costume riding by on his bike, the handwritten sign at the concession stand that reads MILK DUDS AVAILABLE ON REQUEST)—which you've been meaning to do for years, a chronicle of that which means to be forgotten. Objects like this retain their future purposes. They'll accompany you to your next destination.

There are also, however, the trickier ones. There are those that are obdurately present, and must be sorted out. There are those that must be here somewhere, and those you'd forgotten entirely. As Robbie sets about packing, as he opens drawers and boxes that exhale their draughts of 2003 or 2011, he worries that these bits of ephemera, shown to a stranger, would not collectively suggest any specific person at all. He wonders if it might be useful, in the future if not today, to make a list.

Inventory

 1. A missing photograph.

The photograph, wherever it is, depicts Robbie and a boy named Zach, college sophomores, standing together in the semi-shade of a campus archway, with a furl of carved limestone flowers hovering over their heads. Zach— tousled, wiry, densely freckled—grins madly, arms thrown around Robbie's shoulders, left leg slung around Robbie's waist (Robbie might be a tree Zach is climbing), as Robbie, who has shed eighteen pounds since high school and acquired a patch of roan-colored beard, stands straight and square-shouldered, practicing the English schoolboy smile which, he hopes, conveys a reserved cordiality (maybe he was too earnestly, eagerly friendly in high school). The photo was taken at the zenith of his romance with Zach, when they were each other's first boyfriends, holding hands all over campus, kissing on the A train, and fuck anyone who didn't like it. When they joked sometimes about their "college gay phase" it seemed categorically untrue to Robbie because they teased each other about it. He thought, then, that teasing was a less incriminating manifestation of deeper fears and desires.

It took a while, afterward—it took quite a while—for Robbie to understand that only he had been in love; that Zach wasn't teasing the day when, at the end of their junior year, he said, *Man, I love you but I'm not really all that into guys, it's not you, this has been an amazing experience I had with you.*

Robbie had been so sure that they were sparring, in the way of young lovers, as a prelude to a future together: an apartment in the East Village, nights of falling into bed, sweat-soaked from dancing, all hopped up for more sex, and more. Robbie had believed that after his own less-than-promising adolescence (the chubby boy, overly solicitous, the disappointing younger brother of his locally famous sister) he'd been rewarded, in college, by early love in the form of a vigorous, rapacious boy who played his own songs of hope and longing on an acoustic guitar, who won Frisbee tournaments, who'd been dating no less a girl than Donna Clarke before he took up with Robbie . . .

For a few years after graduation, Robbie heard snatches of news. Zach had married a dancer from Canada, Zach had moved to Amsterdam, Zach was in town but hadn't called.

Those years were Robbie's first experience of himself as a memory—a figure who'd entered and exited, somebody's gay phase, remembered fondly, but (this seemed impossi-

ble, given all that they'd said and done) unmourned, rele-
gated, a story from Zach's colorful past.

Robbie misses this particular photo more than any of the
others, which he keeps in a blue leatherette-bound album.
This absent picture strikes him especially as inarguable evidence. Something did occur. Vows were exchanged, if un-
spoken. For obscure reasons (maybe because Robbie can't
seem to find it) this picture is imbued with the nimbus surrounding the moment it was taken: the sex he and Zach
had had less than an hour before, in Robbie's dorm room,
where Robbie bottomed for the first time; Berta the big
rowdy girl who'd taken the picture (*You two are like fucking Tristan and Isolde, if you happen to have heard of them*);
that evening's showing of *Psycho Beach Party* and the sex he
and Zach had had after the movie in an alley a few blocks
from the theater, quick and furtive, standing up, which
seemed at the time to have cured Robbie forever of his own
burden of nervous obedience, which subsequently grew
back, surprisingly quickly.

Robbie is sure the photograph will turn up. He can't
have thrown it away. It's probably stuck between the pages
of a book. Robbie has always used whatever's closest to
hand as a bookmark. He found a desiccated marigold once,
in *Anna Karenina,* and a decade-old electric bill in *The
Magic Mountain.* Someday he'll open an old copy of a book
he hasn't read since college and the picture will come tumbling out. He feels sure about that.

2. Medical school letters.

Acceptances from Duke, NYU, Cornell, and Stanford, re-
jections from Harvard, Yale, and Michigan. Robbie keeps

them in a manila envelope as . . . what, exactly? Still more evidence? Robbie never looks at the letters, never removes them from the envelope, not even when he moves, but has kept them, possibly against the day no one believes he ever turned down medical school in order to teach sixth grade, or just because throwing them away, worthless as they are, might inspire in him, decades from now, a disbelief in the choice he made, the future he foreclosed, not (or so he thinks, most days) due to regret but because, as far as he knows, few people are ever offered this much clarity: walk through the door, or don't walk through the door. It will make a difference. It might make more difference than you realize, at the time.

3.   A cashmere scarf.

Luminously smoky blue, a color that seems to exist only in Italy, from Peter after he'd hurried back from his meeting in Geneva to be on time for Robbie's twenty-fifth birthday. It must have cost a fortune. In retrospect, the scarf strikes Robbie as the true beginning of the end, with Peter. The scarf was, is, formally beautiful and utterly uneccentric, dignified, in the way of expensive objects. It was so wrong that it might have been intended for someone else, not at any rate for Robbie, who wore Carhartt jeans and thrift-store flannel shirts and his father's old overcoat which retained, subtly, the memory of sweat and Old Spice.

The scarf was well intended. Peter had committed no crime of love. He'd been rushed. He'd left the conference a day early in honor of Robbie's birthday and had probably chosen the least-unsuitable birthday present among the offerings at the Geneva airport.

It might have been better if Peter had offered the scarf with some undertone of apology (*best I could do, kid, let's go shopping for your real birthday present tomorrow*) instead of carrying through on his own bluff (*you think maybe it's time to start dressing like an adult?*). They'd tacitly agreed, until then, to hyperbolic, faux-bitter jokes about the fact that Peter was twenty years older (*I never had sex with Abraham Lincoln, not that he wasn't into it*) (*do you want to dance or are you afraid you'll fall and break a hip*). Remarks like those suited them. They ceded the advantage to Robbie's youth, which was a considerable asset but needed bolstering when Peter, without comment, picked up the dinner tabs and paid for the taxis.

But here was the wildly expensive scarf, offered without irony, because (Robbie supposes) Peter was embarrassed about having lost track of Robbie's birthday or because Peter actually meant it about dressing like an adult. Robbie doesn't blame him for that. How long would anyone want to be taken, by waiters and desk clerks, for Robbie's father? Robbie dutifully wore the scarf along with the graphite-colored Lanvin jacket Peter bought him for Christmas, which helped make the scarf look less ludicrous on him but did not help him feel less like the petulant ungrateful child he seemed to have become. Although he didn't leave Peter for almost another year, the scarf was, it seems, the beginning of the end.

Robbie has kept it, though, rolled up at the back of a dresser drawer. He did love Peter, or thought he did. Robbie still flinches at Peter's weary acceptance of his own suspicion that a twenty-five-year-old would drop him eventually; at Peter's wistful gratitude for a few good years, an appallingly elderly-sounding phrase for a man who hadn't yet turned forty-six. The scarf has become a memento mori of sorts, in remembrance of the still-disquieting suggestion that, by forty-six, a man has already entered the age of gratitude. Robbie also keeps the scarf, more obscurely, because he might, even now, become someone who would unselfconsciously wear something so exquisite, so ostentatiously costly, so adult.

4. A boarding pass.

Miami to LaGuardia, November 20, 2010. He would, according to his calculations, have been flying over North Carolina or Virginia. His mother's demise was expected. Its suddenness was not.

Robbie doesn't blame himself. Isabel didn't make it, either. Robbie can, when he chooses to, blame their father, who could have called two or three hours earlier than he did—their father being convinced that their mother might still recover, even after she'd lapsed into her final sleep—but there's no real satisfaction in it, blaming a man too fragile and too desolate for recrimination to be of much help. Robbie prefers blaming his father for his modesty of being, for his monkish remove, for his refusal to fight with Robbie and Isabel's mother even at her most withering and tyrannical, for being as much a third child as he was a husband and father. Robbie does reproach him for the fact that their mother's hospital bed was already empty by the time he and Isabel got there (ready for its next occupant), for a handshake and a clap on the shoulder in lieu of the embrace reserved for Isabel, for the posthumous gift of their mother's Montblanc pen which Robbie meant to keep, he did mean to keep it, can't tell when he left it in a bank or a library or wherever but, unlike the old photograph, he's certain that his mother's pen is no longer anywhere on the premises.

5. Everything.

There is nothing here that Adam didn't touch, in one way or another.

6. Nothing.

There is nothing here that Oliver *did* touch, though he came over on any number of days and nights. He is, however, gone, without a trace.

The park is still wintry, its grass sere and its trees bare. Atop the rise ahead, fully visible through the leafless trees, stands the tower of the Prison Ship Martyrs Monument, under which (so says Google) lie the bones of uncountable Revolutionary War dead.

Dan and Garth walk abreast on a gently sloping uphill path, with Odin murmuring in the snuggly Garth wears slung over his chest and Violet several paces ahead, performing spins and arabesques with feigned abandon when she expects to be congratulated for her grace, to be assured of her future as a dancer, destined to play singing princesses on Broadway stages. The dog run lies some distance ahead. There's no telling yet whether or not the white Chihuahua will be there with its owner, a portly, bearded man who permits Violet to exclaim over the dog but reminds her not to pet it because, as he puts it, she's a biter. Neither the man nor Violet was amused when Garth said, on their first meeting, "No worries, Violet's a biter, too."

Dan says to Garth, "Seems like you and Chess are going to have to work something out."

Garth bounces Odin gently in the snuggly, does not look at Dan. "I was five minutes late."

"You didn't show up at all last week."

"Uh, that was more like three weeks ago."

"Still."

"I texted. I didn't just not show up."

"You should talk. You and Chess. That's all I'm saying."

A runner, a middle-aged man in a black skullcap and a black down vest, jogs by, neatly sidestepping Violet, who is in mid-twirl.

Garth says, "How about we let me take care of this one on my own?"

"Absolutely."

"Chess and I *are* working it out."

"I'm sure you are," Dan says.

Dan takes a sour satisfaction in disapproving of Garth. Dan's disapproval is like a sore knee or a stiff neck, a mild enough pain that evolves, over time, from affliction to contrary but reliable companion.

Dan and Garth once were high school desperados, offhandedly handsome in their motorcycle boots and ragged jeans, their slouchy knowingness and their never-washed tangles of hair, their shared quality of jaded unconcern. The Byrne brothers. If one of them doesn't break your heart, the other one will.

The irony, over the longer term: Garth is the uncontested winner of their childhood bad-boy competition, the one who's never yet listened to reason, who accepts no responsibility, who perceives himself as an elusive goat-footed figure playing pipes for a child to whom he has no legal rights; Garth who waits for his art to be taken up and venerated although no one of influence seems yet to have stopped into the gallery, while Dan— who shouted lyrics into rooms full of fans, who acquired a sufficiently respectable body of addictions to spend three months in rehab—has pulled himself together. Dan has established his own private inner museum of Garth's missteps, his bunglings, his overestimations of his own powers. The DUI, the unpaid loans, the seven-month marriage to that poor turbulent unschooled girl, the second DUI. Dan is the museum's curator, and its sole visitor.

The nature of the competition has shifted. Dan is the handsome boy who married the forceful, not-quite-beautiful girl of whom others disapproved—as Garth put it, *Dude I've got a few crazy-hot girls for you if you think you're running low.* Dan is the guy better able to see that which was, and still is, invisible to Garth. Dan was, is, the brother who would not spend his life with a vacuous crazy-hot girl whose hotness would have faded with time and left in its wake a woman who didn't contemplate, who could express only affection or rage, who'd learn to despise Garth for his own fading interest in her until it was time for the divorce which (there's this, at least) Garth had the sense to instigate sooner rather than later. Dan does maintain a lurking, perverse envy of the unallayed fury she hurled at Garth, all the more so because the fire she set did little more than blacken two of the walls and melt the beatific face of Garth's Taiwanese Buddha, which remains today in Garth's apartment, its hands still joined prayerfully, its head a charred, socketed lump.

Isabel is a reasonable person. Isabel is not insane. Isabel is a serious, thoughtful woman, subject to fits of discontent but never self-righteous, never malicious or destructive or, for that matter, prone to tight, spangly, low-cut dresses worn to obscure performance pieces or art openings that did not favor spangles or cleavage. Dan can't say when, exactly, he realized he'd expected Isabel to be grateful. He'd rather not know about the extent of his own vanity, the hubris that led him to marry a woman he thought would be glad about his eagerness to marry her at all, he who was a fledgling rock star, who'd been asked more than once to autograph a fan's bare breast. He who defiantly married a remarkable if outwardly unspectacular woman.

He's done his best to atone. He went into rehab, for the coke and the drinking and a few pharmaceuticals he's never mentioned to anyone. He broke up his band, stopped writing music altogether. He volunteered to be a househusband for a while so she could devote herself to her own career. He became, to the best of his ability, an affable, uncomplaining person who made the formula, first for Nathan and then for Violet; who did diapers and laundry; who had dinner ready when Isabel came home at night, tired and depleted; the husband who asked faithfully, *How was your day* and listened when she narrated her body of trials and triumphs, her high-strung erratic boss, the brilliant young photographers she'd discovered, the envies and sabotages practiced by Janelle and Avery and the others, who could not comprehend how Isabel got better story assignments—Isabel who would soon be promoted because she was (*Dan, I can only say this to you*) more gifted than any of them.

He's not quite sure when he edged over from acting like an affable, harmless man and *became* an affable, harmless man. It seems to have occurred by imperceptible degrees.

And this, by way of surprises: Isabel appreciates the man Dan has transformed himself into but is not all that interested in him.

It's time, then, for him to start writing music again. It's time for him to reclaim himself, even if he doesn't get beyond playing the occasional skanky club. Even if he finds himself booked in a Mexican restaurant.

Please don't let it be a Mexican restaurant.

Forty isn't too late. He hopes it isn't too late.

dam was the third, between Peter and Oliver. Adam was the one who left marks, who was (as Robbie sees, belatedly) the reason Robbie thought it might be a good idea to date Oliver.

Robbie picks up another essay. Deirdre Matthias, the girl who sits in front and raises an eager hand in response to Robbie's every question (*Me, call on me*). Deirdre's opening line: "As a princess I knew I was destined to marry the person who stood so proudly at the bow of the ship."

At the top of the page Robbie writes, with a red felt-tipped pen, *I wish her luck with that! A.*

Before reaching for the next essay he thinks, can't help thinking, of a night several years ago, when he was a princess in the guise of a man, destined or so he'd thought to marry the person who stood at the bow of the ship.

It was April, here, in this apartment. Robbie and Adam lay together in Robbie's bed. They'd had sex. They'd both undergone what they called the *bottom-ification* process. They'd been tops when they met. It was awkward until Robbie, then Adam, found that their desires were powerful enough to lead them (first Robbie, then Adam) to become, in Grindr-speak, more versatile.

On that April night, Adam was already asleep, his face pressed into Robbie's armpit. Among Adam's virtues: he appreciated all Robbie's bodily humors, the sweets and the sours, the armpit sweat. The appreciation was mutual.

That said, Robbie was always searching Adam's body for what he thought of as Adam's ur-smell, that which could be bottled in a glass vial labeled *Adam*. As far as Robbie could tell, Adam was not engaged in a similar hunt for Robbie's essence. Adam was an audience for Robbie's body, not an explorer. Adam took it as it came. He was not trying to ferret out Robbie's . . . Robbie-ness.

Which was fine. Men brought their differences. It was probably fine.

Robbie, in bed with the slumbering Adam, was able to stare at him, which was not permitted while Adam was awake. An unexpected quality of Adam's: he was chagrined by his own prettiness. He worried that he was not who he appeared to be, that the being within the body could only disappoint.

Robbie had never dreamt that anyone who looked like Adam might harbor ambiguity of any kind. The distant apparitions—the perfect men he saw, jogging through Washington Square Park or dancing in a club or standing in line at a Starbucks—looked so complete unto themselves, so effortlessly well-favored, members of a biological aristocracy who may very well have been kind and courteous but who were still, always, speaking to others from their own parallel, more bountiful worlds. Robbie tried not to dwell overmuch on speculations about any attachment on Adam's part to Robbie's own less orthodox beauty. Did Adam find sanctuary in it? Did Robbie offer release from Adam's sense of his own obligation to be unrelentingly attractive, all the time?

Don't overthink it, okay?

Because there was Adam, somnolent, fully available for viewing. There was his tousle of deep-blond hair, the patrician apostrophe of his nose, his lushly heavy lips.

Robbie was taken then by a tremor of love, for Adam's gentle and uneasy soul, his devotion to the cello which stood in a corner of Robbie's bedroom like an infinitely patient parent, keeping watch through the night.

Robbie touched Adam's hair, softly, so as not to awaken him. Adam's hair was springy but finely spun, a nimbus of dark gold that sent tendrils of brighter gold down onto his forehead. Robbie thought about the unknowable dream that was finding its way into Adam's mind, just then.

Was it a sign of love when you genuinely wanted to hear about another person's dreams? It seemed that it must be.

This was love, then. It had finally arrived. How could Robbie ever have harbored fears about never finding it? He'd seen the expressions on Dan's and Isabel's faces the night Adam was persuaded to play the Bach cello suite for them. He'd witnessed their witnessing of his own happiness, which only compounded it, delivered it back to Robbie, magnified, made unutterably real.

It wouldn't be until late July when Adam told Robbie, stammeringly and tearfully, about the young violinist he'd met. As of that April night, Robbie would feel impossibly fortunate for almost another three months.

He finds, almost two years later, as he's packing up, that there's nothing of Adam's to take with him.

He has to stop packing and get through the remaining Columbus essays. He's got less than two hours.

Sonia Thomas's is still on the top of the pile. "We thought that that man in the big boat was bringing us magic." Robbie writes at the top of the page, *Everybody loves magic! A.* He eats a Cheeto.

Next is Sam Schneider, possessed already of a wry sense of humor, a kid whose allure will be more widely apparent when he's in college, playing to a more sophisticated audience. Sam's opening line: "Bamboozled again! I guess we didn't learn our lesson when we sold the island for a few strands of beads."

The chronology is off by about two centuries. Robbie should follow up with Sam about that. He will. Eventually, he will. For now, though, he writes at the top of the page, *Worst real estate deal in history! A.*

On to the next essay. He eats another Cheeto.

It's unconscionable to pay such scant attention to the kids. It's increasingly impossible to do otherwise.

Time to think about looking for another line of work, just as it's time to find another place to live. So many have lived in these attic rooms and departed, from the indentured Irish girls to whoever it was who painted the place that orangey brown to whoever it was who thought maybe a skylight would help. Now it's Robbie's turn. Cardboard cartons, still empty, are stacked against the wall behind the love seat in the living room/dining room/kitchen, but that's all Robbie has gotten to, so far. He can't seem to start packing up until he knows where he's going next.

River view. Wait and see about that.

He should not be single, looking for a semi-affordable apartment, at the age of thirty-seven. He should not be hoping that "river view" will prove to mean, at least, a sliver of the Hudson glistening between what will inevitably be the buildings across the street. At this price, that's as good as it's likely to be.

He may rent it anyway, if it isn't too awful. He's all too familiar with what's out there, in his price range, and he can't put it off too much longer. He could rent the apartment and give notice at work and . . . do something else. Find another career. Find another boyfriend.

It's time to abandon a life of reasonable expectations. It's time to be more interesting to himself. It's time to find his own Wolfe, in whatever form Wolfe takes. Robbie has begun to understand that by inventing a person and summoning him every day, he's imbued him with the rudimentary aspects of a soul or, if "soul" isn't the right word (there are those discouraging, unsexy Catholic associations), a beingness that exceeds Wolfe's details and his days. A quality Robbie suspects he'll be able to see in just about any man. Neither beauty nor noble profession is required.

Dan is right—it's time to get back on the horse. Or, maybe more accurately, it's time to find a horse he can imagine riding all the way to the horizon, and beyond.

Derrick scowls over the photographs laid out on the far end of the table: a scrappy-looking bearded guy, grinning madly, wearing round wire-rimmed Trotsky eyeglasses, standing beside an abundant red-haired Asian woman wearing a scoop-necked navy blue T-shirt and a benign if startled expression. Between them their two-year-old daughter, who appears, in all four shots, in all three locations (kitchen, living room, front yard), to be nervously pleased, as if she's been given something—a toy, a treat—she's not usually permitted.

Derrick, considering the pictures, says, "I just think he's made them look too much like everybody else."

Amber tells him, "They *are* like everybody else."

Isabel slips Amber a grateful glance. Amber is, after all, not nervous about incurring Derrick's fit of indignant self-defense, since Amber is already looking for another job. Isabel has yet to tell Derrick about that.

Derrick nods to indicate that he's heard Amber, but does not look at her. It's his custom, when he receives an opinion he dislikes, to act as if an irritating, disembodied voice has mysteriously sounded from somewhere within his own head.

He says, staring at the images, "I know they're like everybody else. I don't want them to look like *freaks*. Does it sound like that's what I'm saying?"

"No, not at all." This from Emilia, who's already found another job. It's her final week here. She's grown more agreeable to Derrick, to everyone, since she's known she's on her way out.

"I only mean—" Derrick pauses. Derrick is possessed of a symmetrical precision of form and gesture. He's widely considered handsome, with his aristocratic slope of nose and his delicately cleft chin. Years ago, Isabel thought of him for Robbie, until she and Derrick went for late drinks at Indochine and Derrick said what he said to the waitress.

"I only mean," he continues, "that this story is about variations, not perfect facsimiles. This story is about extending the boundaries of families. Does that make sense?"

"Yeah, it completely does," Emilia offers.

When Amber adds, "How much variation do you have in mind?," she makes no attempt to veil her sarcasm.

Amber and Emilia are, in their way, studies in the leave-taking strategies of children even if, at the ages of twenty-four and twenty-seven, they are thoroughly grown. Some children want to be fondly remembered. Others want to make sure they can never return.

For Isabel, it's a sign of her own age that, on one hand, Amber and Emilia and the other kids in the photo department are distinguishable—it's not difficult to tell a Long Island cheerleader from a Mexican girl who may never recover from Harvard—but, on the other, that she, Isabel, can only see them, collectively, as *young*. They can only strike her as nascent, on their way into futures in which they'll be . . . who knows what or who they'll be, beyond the promise that they will not be assistant photo editors at a magazine, will not work for a magazine at all, since magazines will, soon enough, cease to exist.

When Isabel started here a dozen years ago, she herself may have struck others as someone whose youth preempted all her other qualities. Someone temporary, passing through this scrim toward the truer life that awaited her.

It's unexpected, then, that Isabel has proven to be permanent, as the magazine is looking more and more temporary. When she was hired it didn't occur to her, not even as the haziest of premonitions, that this magazine—this avatar of stylishness and design—would fade along with most of the others, or that she, a decade-plus into her own future, would find herself still here, qualified only for a job that will soon no longer be a job at all, too well paid to do anything but continue showing up until the day she and the remaining staff arrive one morning to find the lobby doors locked.

It's time for her to speak. She seems to have lost track of herself. What, after all, does she, the senior photo editor, think about the idea of *variation*?

She says, "Why don't I ask Juan for more options?"

It's not the level of problem-solving for which she's paid what she's paid. It is, however, the only answer to the question, and she's the one to deliver it.

Derrick nods. He says, "I wouldn't mind seeing everything Juan shot."

"I'll talk to him about that."

Isabel knows—Derrick knows too, but is less encumbered by the possible—that Juan will refuse to show them *everything*. Juan has already sent his choices. Isabel might be able, at best, to cajole him into letting her see a half dozen or so of the runners-up, among which there might be—there will be— a few that are just off-kilter enough to satisfy Derrick's wish for two trans parents who look ever so slightly less like everybody else, and yet not too *unlike* everybody else.

First there'll be the matter of getting more images from Juan, a request he'd have refused outright as recently as a year ago. Work is drying up for him, along with everyone else. Second will be Isabel's battle with Derrick about using one or two of the less flattering shots, the ones Juan held back. Juan always prefers glamour, which is why Isabel chose him for this story, but Derrick has caught her out. It seems likely that these people, this couple who live defiantly in a New Jersey suburb, who've agreed to be photographed by a magazine, will come out looking a little less like everybody else because they'll look a little less attractive than most people whose pictures appear in magazines.

Isabel is confident that after they'd agreed to the shoot they debated over what to wear, about whether or not he should trim his beard, because they were happy about the prospect of looking like everybody else. Which, as they may be shocked to learn, is precisely what the magazine does not want.

Isabel would, once, have argued with Derrick about the very notion of asking Juan for more photos. She'd have argued too, assuming Juan sends the photos at all, in favor of letting this scrappily unusual family look as pretty as they hope to. But it's not ten o'clock yet and she's already imagined seeing an owl, she's already wept on the subway. Derrick has already moved farther down the table, to frown over the spread on Astoria.

As Dan and Garth walk along the path in the park, Garth bounces the baby (a trifle too roughly, should Dan mention it?), says, "Hey there, mini-man."

Dan is taken by a tremor of scorn twisted up with painful affection, as if they were two names for the same emotion. Walking alongside Garth through the sun-dappled chill of the park, Dan is briefly bushwhacked by a vertiginous love-fury that blows out at Garth and slams right back into him, a storm of emotion that encompasses them both. Garth the narcissistic fuckup, but Dan, too—Dan the luckier brother, the one who's learned to live within reason, and found comfort there. Dan whose life rests on a foundation more substantial than optimism and his own allure. Dan will not feel vindicated as Garth's sparks start sputtering out, as Chess revokes his limited parenthood and the gallery drops him and people start saying, *He used to be handsome, you know.* Dan will be good for a loan and a place to crash but he'll know, he'll always know, that Garth is his to love and revile, the brother who ended up missing out on everything because he couldn't help being five minutes late, who always had an explanation and couldn't comprehend how or why that didn't matter. The two walk quietly together as Violet points to the dog run, which is still distant, still only a chain-link fence surrounding small canine blurs of movement, as she says, "I think I see the white dog already," as Garth calls to her, "Hey, there's a whole world of dogs out there," as Violet executes a Broadway-star twirl for Garth's benefit and Garth urges her on. Garth, Dan's second self, the irresponsible brother, the ever-so-slightly handsomer one, the boy who could talk his way out of pretty much anything because who, really, wasn't at least a little bit in love with him? Garth at thirty-eight, though, has been practicing his seductions long enough for the effort to show. Garth is running out of time. Garth is running out of luck. Garth is loved, truly loved, by only one person. Garth is Dan's to suffer and censure, to blame, to defend. To helplessly and angrily adore.

D errick isn't pleased by the photos of Astoria (the latest *it* neighborhood), which, as Derrick puts it, doesn't look very *it* in these pictures, with its take-out joints and discount stores, its row houses sheathed in brick-patterned tar paper, even if Jacob the photographer did catch a Medusa-haired skateboard kid with a mouthful of gold teeth and a youngish woman in a Pucci dress carrying a bag of Chinese takeout.

Isabel can only nod in mute agreement and try to look concerned. She knew Jacob would search out the subtler signs, just as she knows what's coming with Derrick. He'll want her to hire a different photographer, someone more clued in, what about Andrea? Isabel will remind him that Andrea only shoots film and they don't have time for that. Derrick will say what about Izzy then, or Roberto, and Isabel will remind him that Izzy and Roberto book a month or more in advance, they're among the few who don't *need* more work these days, they're not going to drop everything to spend a day shooting in Astoria. Derrick will feel confident that they'll do it for *him*. Isabel will be compelled to find yet another way of reminding Derrick that the new budget has cut deeply into his capacity to snap his fingers and make things happen. He'll turn on her. (*All right, so where are the hot, hungry new talents you're supposed to be finding?*) She'll find a way or won't find a way of saying, once again, that she's looking for new talent all the time but,

Derrick, you have no idea how many new talents aren't all that eager to climb aboard a sinking ship, which will elicit either rage (*We're not dead yet, sweetheart*) or abjection (*I'm turning fifty this year, five-oh*) or both. Isabel will do her best to placate him. She cares about Derrick, she doesn't not care about Derrick, even after he made that remark to the waitress. She respects him, up to a point. He occupies the narrow, shifty zone between culture and corruption. He calls forth a dowager grandeur in his wide-ranging disapprovals (picnics, any roses other than white, the entire nation of France) and his intractable convictions: Edward Hopper (overrated), Japanese antiques (underappreciated), the sexiness of a string of pearls on pretty much anyone. Derrick is, at least, a true devotee—to art, to fashion, to manners and money.

Still, he's extinguishing Isabel's on-the-job capacity for generating what might be called joy but, more accurately, should probably be thought of as the scouring away of sorrow. It's increasingly possible for Isabel—who loved her job until the day she didn't, it seems to have been almost that abrupt—to fall into states of sluggish, low-grade anxiety whenever she's with Derrick, who refuses to apprehend a future in which he'll be a person of lesser consequence. As Derrick begins to recede (how can he fail to see it?), to surrender not only his limitless budget but the heightened, extravagant world he's been inventing for more than two decades, he takes with him Isabel's own professional ferocity, her intricate mix of concurrence and opposition. She's been the one who discovers marginal young photographers and manages, one way or another, to seduce them into giving her their own takes on the magazine's lambent, Vermeer-ish look, its anti-glamour glamour (*Would you shoot another roll with less light, let's try her in the gray taffeta, with no makeup at all*). She's been the one to wage the battles, to assert that *this* revivifying neighborhood is displacing too many people or *that* handbag line is so expensive as to cross over from the luxurious into the grotesque (*Derrick, we're not doing that story, period*). But as the money vanishes, as Isabel's work turns by degrees into a job that requires forbearance over combat, as Derrick joins the ranks of endangered species, Isabel has to resist her own desire, many days, to curl up under her desk and take a nap.

She's about to talk Derrick into the images of Astoria they've got already, to convince him that there's neither the time nor the budget for new ones and really isn't it a little *obvious* to run images of the single good restaurant and the rigorously curated vintage shop, both of which will probably be gone six months from now? She'll nurse Derrick through his anger or his bitter acquiescence, hoping for anger, which is less heartbreaking than the petulant laments to which he's increasingly prone. Before she launches her riff, though—before she attends to him, before she gets him through *this one*—she thinks again about trains, about the destinations board at Grand Central, about the women who abandon everything, every burden and expectation, every hope . . .

Dobbs Ferry
Manitou
Cold Spring
Jewel, or Marcia, or Antoinette.

The white Chihuahua is absent from the dog run.

There are hardly any dogs at all: a disheveled gray mixed breed that chases and retrieves, chases and retrieves the red rubber ball thrown distractedly by the dog's owner as she speaks angrily into her cellphone; a miniature schnauzer standing stationary, confused, as if it knows something is expected of it but can't tell what; and an elderly dachshund curled up on itself in the lee of a bench, ignoring the imprecations of a small boy who wants the dachshund to get up and frolic.

Violet says, "The white one isn't here."

"I think maybe she comes in the afternoons," Dan says. "We don't usually come here in the morning."

Garth says, "Looks like you've got other prospects, though."

Violet is not interested in other prospects. She loves only the little white dog.

Dan asks the woman throwing the ball for the shaggy gray dog if his daughter can throw the ball. The woman hands it to Dan without looking at him or pausing in her argument with whomever. Dan hears the woman say, ". . . if that's your idea of collectible . . ." and moves quickly away, lest she suspect him of an ulterior motive (*Hey, I've got a five-year-old daughter, right here*), but when Dan proffers the ball to Violet, she refuses it. The gray dog, a chaotic ungraceful animal, barks and scuffles and leaps—*throw the ball throw the ball throw the ball*—until

Dan throws the ball himself. The dog scurries after it as Garth settles with Odin onto the farther, unoccupied bench. As Garth whispers to Odin and Dan throws the ball again for the dog, and again, Violet goes to the waist-high fence that surrounds the dog run, where she stands facing out over the park, with its meandering pathways and its licorice-stick lampposts, its brittle wintry bushes. The white dog must be coming. If Violet waits long enough, she knows it will appear, straining at the end of its leash. She knows that when she first spots it it will look like a speck of light on the broad brown slope of the park, hurtling toward her.

R obbie picks up the next essay. Roger Ross. This one will be virtually incomprehensible. Robbie puts the essay down and takes up his phone.

Image: A farm stand in a place that could be Vermont, with an unsmiling old woman standing behind a profusion of daffodils and hyacinths in white plastic buckets.

Wolfe and Lyla have driven farther north. Maybe they'll buy that house. Maybe they won't. Maybe the house won't appear on Instagram again. Maybe it was nothing more than a fleeting impulse, already forgotten. Wolfe's followers don't insist on narrative coherence, any more than they insist on the persistence of memory.

Caption: The flowers are out already. Who knew? I think we're going to buy all of them, fill up the car. I think we're going to keep driving.

Maybe Wolfe and Lyla will drive all the way to Canada. Maybe they'll abandon their lives, which are rich and full but nevertheless . . .

What about Montreal, where Robbie has never been but has always vividly envisioned: a city of glittering ice palaces, a place where people skate to their jobs on frozen rivers, where lovers hold each other in candlelit rooms, under hillocks of quilts and comforters, where the shade of Leonard Cohen lingers in front of the church of Our Lady of the Harbor, singing "Suzanne" softly to himself. Who wouldn't want to load up the car with daffodils and hyacinths and keep driving, all the way to Montreal?

April 5, 2020

Afternoon

Wolfe_man

Image: A harbor so extravagantly blue as to suggest a glistening serenity uncompromised by the presence of human beings, although there is a sailboat, a pristine white triangle in the middle distance, and the finger of a lighthouse so far away it appears to float on the horizon. The boat and the lighthouse, along with the water and the sky, could be properties of an afterlife that mimics the earthly works of mortals (boats, lighthouses) but has also prepared for us a rarefied incarnation of that which we knew on earth, that which we knew to *be* the earth, a vastness intended to inspire both consolation and awe, as if the two were variations on a single human response.

Caption: Iceland. Even after a few months it still feels more like it's been bestowed on us, like it recognizes us, instead of a place where we're just visiting as tourists.

Isabel, sitting on the stairs, hopes she's not staring at the image on her phone with an expression that could reasonably be called frightening intensity, were anyone to see her. She hopes she has not become a frighteningly intense person, though it can be difficult to know about that, as it's become difficult to know about many things.

She is—why deny it?—frighteningly intense about Robbie and Wolfe. She does her best to conceal it from Dan and the kids. She checks Instagram only when she's alone out here on the stairs.

Although she knows better, she can't seem to overcome her conviction that Robbie has left her for Wolfe and that Wolfe has left her for Robbie, as well.

She's slightly frighteningly intense because she's at least somewhat delusional. In her right(er) mind she knows she has not been discarded or shunted aside. Still, the delusion persists. Robbie has laid claim to Wolfe, Robbie has fled with Wolfe to Iceland (*Iceland*) and left her behind to take care of . . . everything that's happening here.

Isabel, in her right mind, reminds herself that Robbie (and Wolfe) have been trapped in Iceland for almost four months, on a trip that was meant to be six weeks. They haven't abandoned her. There's simply the fact of the now-uncrossable Atlantic, flights grounded until further notice, two thousand seven hundred miles of water between there and here.

Still, she's spending more and more time with her phone, on the stairs. There's no other place in the apartment in which to be alone. There is, occasionally, an unoccupied room, but it's never long before Violet approaches her with questions and complaints or Dan asks if she'll listen to the lyrics of another new song or Nathan comes downstairs to keep her informed about his triumphs at League of Legends.

Even here, though, she's never quite safe from interruptions, from her family's need for her to listen with patient interest to the fears and grievances, the victories or the songs, along with their need to be in the vicinity of a person who knows more than anyone else about what to do and not do in order to be safe, who knows with unwavering assurance that everything will be all right.

She is not entirely sure about what's safe, and is even less sure that everything will be all right. Still, she offers that. If she doesn't, no one else will.

Robbie would. But Robbie is in Iceland.

Isabel pictures the future residents of the apartment, passing her on the stairs as they come and go, living as they do in a world in which coming and going is natural again. It's important to believe that coming and going will be natural again, that the denizens of the future will think nothing of going out to pick up a few things at the store.

In the future, assuming that there is one, the new people might guess that the woman on the stairs has been misused in some way. Aren't the spectral women in stories usually doomed to linger, searching, bereft, because they've been deceived and abandoned? And really, why wouldn't Robbie betray her with Wolfe, she who'd eaten his birthday cake the night before his second birthday, who'd blamed him for crushing the crayon (aquamarine) into the carpet when he was five, who'd fed him such a relentless diet of misinformation—all the ways you can call bad luck down upon yourself (stepping on an ant, seeing a white cat after dark), the ghost in the garage, the family that lived secretly in the crawl space—that she may (she hopes this, too, is delusional) have helped to create the eccentric child who grew to be the discomfited high school boy with only one friend, a kid (she forgets his name) who spoke, whenever possible, in rhyming couplets; the Robbie who became, ultimately, a grown man who belonged more to her than he did to any of his boyfriends; the Robbie who turned down his medical school acceptances and took a vow of schoolteacherly poverty instead; Robbie the thirty-eight-year-old man-child who'd still be living upstairs if he could; the spinsterish figure Isabel has always (admit it) intended him to be . . .

. . . until the day arrived, too undramatic to be rightfully called *the day* at all, but whenever it was, the *time* after Robbie had moved into the apartment in Washington Heights (Isabel encouraged him to keep looking; *he* was the one who rushed into it), the day or week or month he knew he could not continue teaching sixth grade, could no longer call forth the compassionate patience required of him. Robbie himself wasn't sure (or, if he was sure, didn't say so to Isabel) when exactly he decided to quit his job and go traveling with his share of the pre-inheritance, the useful if unspectacular sum their father elected to give them while he's still alive, a gesture that, coming from their father (who gives hotel shampoo sets as gifts, who keeps old batteries in the belief that they'll regenerate), must mean either that he's eager to see how his children misspend their legacy or that he hasn't yet told them about some new, dire warning from Dr. Meer.

But here, for whatever reason, is Isabel and Robbie's inheritance, given before the mortal fact. Isabel put her share into the kids' college fund. Robbie used his to move out of the apartment in Washington Heights, to quit his job and reapply to medical schools, as if there'd been some miscommunication about his refusals and he was following up, fifteen years later. He used his share to go to Iceland for what was supposed to be six weeks because, as he put it, it would be too weird to be unemployed, waiting for medical schools to respond while still living in that apartment, with its windowless bedroom and its sliver of the Hudson, a hint of shimmer, semi-visible on the brightest days.

Robbie was this person, and then he was that. He became, unexpectedly, someone who wanted to spend time in, as he put it, an inhabited silence, a place where water and stars matter more than they do in New York.

Robbie, as it turns out, is the one who got on the train.

Isabel would like to be happier for him. She'd prefer not to ask herself if, once Robbie was compelled to leave the upstairs apartment, he'd been pressed into an ever-increasing series of leave-takings: Washington Heights (she *did* urge him to keep looking) to Iceland to, soon enough, a medical school in Boston, Baltimore, or Seattle.

Isabel dislikes her own suspicion that Robbie is leaving her, by degrees—that once she and Dan asked him to find another place to live, he began telling them, in a barely decipherable under-language, *Sure, no problem, I'll go far away, I'll go very far away.*

She dislikes feeling abandoned to her own life, here in the apartment. She dislikes herself for feeling cheated, left behind . . .

All the more so as Dan recedes, as he relinquishes his domestic good spirits and grows more emotionally febrile, more withdrawn. As it falls to Isabel to reassure, to listen, to act as if she herself is unafraid.

As those future owners will say, passing her on the stairs: *She keeps staring at that phone, the poor thing; we don't know if she knows that the charge went out long ago, that she's staring at a blank screen.*

Robbie stands at the threshold of the cabin, with the door propped open. It's his favorite spot. With one foot on the floor of the cabin he can maintain his bearings, his sense of domestic scale as he sets his other foot out onto the edge of the immensity: the valley that slopes downward among the pinnacles, fists and spires of rock, treeless but covered everywhere in grass, a seamless carpet that runs uninterrupted to the tops of the escarpments and into their vales and crevasses, as if some god of the North had waved a titanic hand and simply said, *Green*. It's difficult not to think of gods here. The landscape is possessed of a summoned quality, heaved up out of the sea like other islands but, unlike other islands, still possessed of its underwater element, still silent, still extending out into what appear to be limitless oceanic depths. The rented cabin has no porch, or stoop, only a pockmarked stone sill nearly a foot high, against which the door closes as securely as a bank vault and which Robbie has mostly learned not to trip over. The stone could be a barrier against the ubiquitous grass, which, if permitted, would creep steadily into the house and begin covering all its surfaces—the floor and the walls, the furniture, the pots and pans, everything. It seems that no one who builds a house here would fail to erect a barrier between the house and the mountain to which it attaches itself, lest the green gain a foothold, and lay claim to the entire house.

There's only the door and two small windows. The windows, it seems, are here because a house requires windows of some sort, and so there are two of them, equally spaced on either side of the door, barely larger than chessboards, with heavy shutters as well as curtains made of some brownish material that resembles fine-grained burlap but is softer than burlap, imbued with a synthetic-velvet sheen that must have been a nod to some sense of refinement, even if the curtains are as opaque as cardboard, and about that color.

It's all devoted to battening down for winter—consider the winters up here—but Robbie suspects, standing half inside and half out, straddling the stone sill, that the cabin's fastness has to do, as well, with the mountains themselves, in all their weathers; with the conviction that some *animus* blows up from the valley and howls (often silently, but still) over the landscape; a livingness without mind or motive beyond its own force, which, though not malevolent, would flatten any human works not secured against it; that the people who built the cabin knew how much, beyond ice storms, it would need to withstand.

Or maybe it's nothing more mysterious than wind and weather. Robbie has been prone to fantasies since he's been here, to premonitions, a sense of fleeting shadowy forms on the periphery of his vision.

It doesn't help that he's off the grid. There will be no posts, no calls or texts or emails, for as long as he remains on the mountain. It's lonely, and it's liberating. He's accountable to no one except Wolfe, who's gone for a hike. Robbie has been tired lately, more prone to naps than explorations, but it's good to know that Wolfe is out there, in all that stern and verdant beauty.

Robbie nods formally to the landscape, steps inside, and closes the heavy wooden door.

To: Robert Walker
Subject: Re: today
From: Isabel Walker

Hi, Robbie,

Last heard from, you were headed for a glacier in Iceland. It's good to know there still ARE glaciers in Iceland.

The Shoe Hospital across the street has been closed for almost three weeks. The mechanical raccoon is frozen with his hammer raised. I've concluded that it absolutely IS a raccoon and not a fox, though I know you're attached to the fox theory.

There are sirens every day, I can hear one now. There's hardly anyone out on the street. The hospitals are full, they don't know what they're going to do with more and more and more people who get sick. The mortuaries are all full.

There are still no letters from any of the med schools but it's still too soon for that, isn't it?

It's gotten hard to keep track of the days. With the new arrangement I don't really separate weekends from week-days, my job has become some kind of membrane that covers every waking hour, which frankly isn't all that bad,

I mean I've still got a job and having a job keeps me from asking if a murder/suicide pact is necessarily such a bad idea. ☺

Congratulations for posting pictures you actually took and haven't stolen from other people (goodbye to your life of crime). The pix are a little old by now, but still.

We're worried about Violet. We're worried about everybody but Violet is acting funny, even for Violet. She thinks all the letters in the alphabet have personalities, which is sweet but there are a few letters she thinks of as evil. M is a good letter, W is a bad one. Which is odd. Right? And she's convinced we need to keep the windows closed all the time.

I wish I could talk to you. I can't help hoping you'll get back on the grid sooner rather than later. The worry-o-meter is set high, these days.

Nathan as you will not be surprised to hear continues to insist that he doesn't give a shit about school, or Dan and me, or anyone except his beloved Chad and Harrison. Which frankly seems like a reasonably healthy reaction.

I kind of hope Nathan is gay. Not that I have any reason to think so. Is that fucked up? I don't just mean it's all right with me if he's gay, I actually hope he is. Option A—most of the men I know seem to be gay, why wouldn't I want my son to be like most of the men I know?

Option B—it's a reprehensible wish on my part to never have to share him with some girl which means I'm a terrible mother and should probably be put in jail.

Whenever you're back on the grid please circle either A or B for me, OK?

As Miss Edie says, I worry that you'll work in an office have children celebrate wedding anniversaries, the world of heterosexual is a sick and boring life. I can barely remember a time when you and I weren't quoting Miss Edie to each other. That was our favorite all-time movie, I guess maybe it still is.

I sometimes want to go upstairs and open the door and say to Nathan the world of heterosexual is a sick and boring life, and then just close the door again. But that would definitely put me in Option B, wouldn't it?

Anyway Nathan is king of the castle, upstairs. He's still mad at us for taking the lock off the door, and turning off the gas, and going up there all the time to make sure he's all right.

It's hard to know what to do, what to say, etc. to Nathan, or to Violet. Or anybody, but especially the kids. Nathan hates going to school online, I have to check on him even more constantly when classes are in session, and of course he hates me for checking on him as constantly as I do.

Violet seems to see it as a TV show but she has the advantage of being in the first grade, with dancing animated letters and puppets teaching each other how to write and etc. For Nathan, sixth-grade classes aren't really a TV show he, or anybody, wants to watch. He's convinced he knows everything already. I don't always have it in me to fight with him about that.

We need to keep them safe plus we're trying not to scare them too much at the same time. I really wish I could talk to you.

I hope Wolfe's followers aren't worried about him, up in that cabin. Probably they're not. I'm the one who worries. But OK five days in the mountains starts to seem like a long time, when it was only supposed to be two.

We here could not be any more ON the grid.

I don't want to say too much. I don't want to intrude on your serenity, up there. Serenity is God knows hard to come by, these days. But Dan and I are going to have to figure something out. For the future. Assuming there is a future. I'm sure being alone together all the time is good for some couples.

Dan and I can't do anything but keep on. It's dangerous to go to the grocery store, good luck looking for a separate place to live plus we can't do that to the kids or to ourselves for that matter.

I have this idea that you and I could move to the country together. I can work remotely from anywhere, med school will be online, I keep thinking about that house Wolfe didn't buy last year.

The world of heterosexual is a sick and boring life.

I really wish I could talk to you. I've said that already, haven't I?

I don't, as noted, want to intrude on your serenity. I just don't want you to be too surprised when you get home. Though I don't suppose it'll be all that much of a revelation for you.

PS. Dan has 230,000 followers. He's a happy man.

Enough. More soon.

Love and XXXOOO

PPS. Here's another siren, this one is really really close.

Garth checks his messages again. Still nothing from Chess.

Focus on the work, then. He's been waiting to tackle *Hamlet*.

It's a headdress, this time. A helmet of sorts modeled on the headdresses worn by Maasai warriors, on display at the Met. Garth's variation, almost finished, is covered in pigskin coated with tar, riddled with crevices into which he's embedded pebbles of broken glass, rhinestones, and teeth. He's found someone online, some ghoul who sells human teeth. He's interspersed them among the glass and the fake diamonds.

He's written on the wall of his studio, with a charcoal stick: *all occasions do inform against me, and spur my dull revenge.*

Fuck yes, vengeful Prince of Denmark.

Garth scrubs at the tar with a wire brush. It has to look worn. It has to look like an ancient object Hamlet would elect to wear when he finally decides that he needs it.

Garth stands back, gives it a good look. He decides against attaching the steel spike to the top, the one he's sawed off an old German helmet bought at a flea market. The Hamlet headgear wants to be compact, skull-like, nothing for an enemy to take hold of, not even a spike. This headdress is all business. Its secrets are barely concealed in its crevices, as if they were bursting through some substratum of royal ceremony and sacrifice. Diamonds and teeth.

It's good. It has force, and menace. Its intentions are well enough concealed. Still, Garth has to tamp down the conviction that it's missing something. He's learned to ignore that— the impulse to keep working, to add, to make it a more shockingly alive incarnation of itself. A sculpture should always look like it's not quite finished. Hack work is *finished*. It's on offer as an object of veneration. It can only stand in rooms or galleries contemplating what it considers to be its own perfection.

Jesse will be horrified. This is the nastiest one yet. Garth started with the romances—*Cymbeline, The Tempest*—and is just now moving on to the tragedies.

Wait until Jesse sees what Garth is thinking about for *Macbeth*. Wait until he sees *King Lear*.

One of the only advantages of working with a small-time dealer: Jesse takes solace in the conviction that his artists are too outré for what he calls *the international art cartel*. It helps that Jesse's family made a fortune manufacturing sliding glass door frames. He doesn't really need to sell anything. Never mind his refrain about championing what he likes to call "artists who live on the edge of total catastrophe."

Jesse, if you want catastrophe, I'll give you catastrophe.

The tar needs more work, more corrosion, before Garth gessoes it. It wasn't easy finding old-stock gesso, far enough past its prime to give everything the merest hint of yellowish unclarity, of aging lacquer that was once meant to preserve but has, over time, conferred upon the object—the painting, the wax fruit—a frozen ongoing life in the land of the dead.

One more go with the scouring brush, then it's time for the gesso.

Before Garth gets back to work, though, he leaves another

voice mail for Chess. "Hey Chess you know who this is, you know how much I want to see you and the kid but I'd be okay just knowing the two of you are okay. You could just text me a yes or a no, if you feel like you can do that. Wait, I don't mean to sound hostile, I'm not hostile, I'm just . . . thinking about you. Okay that's enough, it's Garth but you know that. Bye."

There's a song inside the song. It isn't beautiful, it isn't *only* beautiful, though it contains beauty like a plum contains its stone. It's the song that leaves nothing out. It's a lament and an aria. It's that old ditty about Frosted Flakes and it's an anthem to the perfume your mother wore when you were a child. It's a hymn sung by girls with candles in paper cups, it's the cry of the rabbit when your father slit its throat, it's the sound of your wife whispering in a dream that's not about you.

Dan hasn't written that song. He can't write it, nobody can, but others have come close. Closer than Dan, so far, at least. What Dan's got is a bouquet of a song, with its minor chord progression that leads unexpectedly into a diminished seventh on the word *spells*.

Which isn't bad. Which is good enough. It's good enough that he does his best not to dwell on the idea of holding a dozen hothouse roses out to the world when he'd hoped to offer an ice pick sharp enough to pierce the skin of the usual, to poke holes in the orderly progression of days.

A surprise: it seems he was more satisfied by the yearning to go back to writing songs than he is now that he's writing them, now that he has two hundred and thirty thousand followers on Instagram and YouTube, now that he's moved from anticipation to a numbed thwarted feeling he doesn't like to call failure. Now that he's able to measure the distances between his ambitions and what he's able to produce. Now that strangers are tweeting about him . . .

WomanFriend 53sec
In Pieces just broke the broken pieces of my heart
Danny I'm not sure if I love u or hate u but anyway don't stop

MarcusMental 1m
This guyz music is SORROW PORN DanSoloSHIT is making a fortune out of our loneliness find ur own happiness instead

DominicDoReMe 2m
laughing and crying u know it's the same release

Zara.zaralynne 3m
If u cant handle emotion u can always sing happy birthday to yourself

TreyvonFreeMan 4m
Could someone tell me why white people love sad songs?

WomanFriend 5m
If you don't like it, you don't have to listen to it. Are you aware of that?

OingoOingoBoing 7m
DANCE DEAD BOY DANCE

Violet doesn't knock, and there's no lock on the door. She seems to think she and Nathan still share a room, that Nathan's new place upstairs is really an extension of the old arrangement, that her right to enter whenever she pleases has not changed.

Nathan is watching *School of Rock* when Violet walks in. He acts as if he doesn't hear or see her. He's glad, at least, that he wasn't jerking off, though it'd serve her right if she found him in the middle of it. That might cure her of barging in.

Violet scans the room. She says, "You're keeping the windows closed."

"Yep."

"Have you done your homework?"

"Why do you care?"

"You're watching that movie *again*?"

"Yep."

Violet settles herself on the sofa beside Nathan with the queenly precision that's ever more how she sits, walks, speaks. She says of Jack Black, "He's so fat."

"Haven't you got something else to do?"

"He's ugly, too. You don't open your windows, do you?"

"This shit doesn't come in through a window."

"Yes it does."

"It's time for you to go back downstairs," he says.

"I'm done with *my* homework."

"So, live your life."

"Why does he sweat so much?"

"He's a rock star. Like Dad used to be."

"Dad isn't fat. Or ugly. Why do you watch this movie so much?"

"I like this movie."

"Can we watch something else?"

"Nope," he says.

"You smell bad."

Nathan does a quick armpit check. The reason for taking showers is . . . what, exactly?

"I need you to leave me alone," he says.

"You open the windows when I'm not here. I can tell."

Nathan muffles the urge to grab her and push her out the door. He could do it. She weighs almost nothing. And all he needs is to be free of her—her condemnations, her infinite self-regard, her disdain for everything that doesn't emanate from her, which means disdain for *everything,* even Jack Black.

Nathan hopes something awful happens to her. He's host to that thought. He retracts it quickly enough—this isn't a time to wish ill fortune on anyone, not even Violet—but the thought has crystallized in his mind, although he dissolved it as quickly as he could.

It's important not to wish harm on anyone. It's important not to wish that the danger will track other people down. You shouldn't even *think* it.

He says, "You don't have to sit here, smelling me."

"I won't."

"Don't."

"I *won't*."

She rises from the couch. "I'll be downstairs," she says.

"I know."

"Tell me when you want to watch something else."

"I'll do that."

Violet goes to the door, turns, and says, "I'll be downstairs."

"Good to know."

She doesn't answer. She merely departs. Nathan knows how she pictures herself: the royal personage taking leave of an impertinent serving boy.

What's most strange: he's glad she's gone, and he wishes she weren't. When she's here, and she's here annoyingly often, there's . . . someone here. Mom and Dad come too, all the time, but they knock first. They can be irritating, Mom with her *Honey, are you all right,* Dad with his *Hey, buddy, you still holding the fort up here?* But there is—it's weird—a bitter and pungent pleasure in the pure rage he can feel toward Violet.

On the TV screen Jack Black plays his guitar, squeezes his face in an expression of ecstatic agony. Jack Black is Nathan's only friend, in the absence of Chad and Harrison. If Nathan concentrates on Jack Black, he can keep, mostly, from hating Violet, from missing her, from thinking that if she were gone he'd be free of hating her, and of missing her. He can have mercy on his parents. He can—it's hardest with Violet, but even with her—keep a lid on his own roil of fury and boredom and thousand-megavolt nervousness, which, if he released it, might roar out of him in what he thinks of as a siren sound but louder, more piercing, a sound so powerful and penetrating it could bring the whole building down.

April 5, 2020

Dear Nathan and Violet,

I'm going to take you to Iceland. When you're older, and everything's back to normal again. It's all grass and stars here. There's a river that'll carry you all the way to the ocean, all you've got to do is float along with the current.

You won't get this letter for a while. Where I am, up in the mountains, there's no post office. There's grass and rivers but no stores or post offices or anything like that. But I'll send it soon, once I've gone back to the civilized world.

When I get back, Nathan, you can beat me at any video game you choose. Violet, we've got to go shopping for some new dresses.

I just want to tell you how much I miss you. I want you to know I'm thinking about you all the time. I know things are hard at home now but that'll get back to normal. I remember normal. I remember you.

Love,
Robbie

For Chess, time has become so innocent of event as to edge into a meditative profundity. The wheels turn on their rails. Wake, breakfast, play, lunch, nap, teach while Odin is napping (hope he doesn't wake up), play, dinner, sleep, repeat. They are each other's only company, if Chess doesn't include her students, and her students don't count as company. They're faces the size of poker chips, in a grid on her computer screen. They're more docile, less argumentative than they were. They bring to their computers a stunned quality, as if they've all been hit with rubber mallets right before class.

The silences are longer and more frequent. Chess is compelled more often to fill them with her own views and convictions, which can be taxing. She's spent years jousting with her students. She hurls her ideas out to younger people who lob them back at her, the more strident students do, and there are always enough of them to make up for the quieter ones. It takes on its own momentum. But this semester, which requires Chess to hold forth largely uncontested . . . it isn't too much trouble, it's only less fun. The students, most of them, are Zooming from their childhood bedrooms, which inspires compassion in Chess. It's important to care about her students but not love them too much.

This year, however, this disembodied semester . . . they've been snatched back to rooms they'd assumed they'd escaped forever. Their childhoods, as it turns out, exert a gravitational

pull none of them had anticipated. Here's Agatha backed by a
Stevie Nicks poster. (How could Agatha, nineteen years old,
know or care about Stevie Nicks?) Here's Rafi seated before an
aquarium in which there appear to be no fish at all; it's only a
glass box full of murky green water. Chess, for her part, has set
herself at her worktable in front of the bookcase. She's done
some editing of the books that stand within visual range. No
reason for the students to know she still owns her childhood
copy of *Winnie-the-Pooh* or, of more recent vintage, the *Lord of
the Rings* trilogy. Nor is there any reason for them to see the
rest of her apartment, which, while filled with the expected
pile upon pile of books, is also testament to her indifference
about furnishings: the white sofa and chairs and end tables
from IKEA (white was on sale), the futon on the floor. Although Chess has lived in this apartment for almost four years,
she hasn't lost her habit of temporality, the sense that she's here
at present but it'd be pointless to settle in, given that she'll be
leaving again. It extends back to her childhood, when she
prayed daily to her mother's statuette of Saint Teresa for rescue, when she left South Dakota for college and graduate
school and from there to her insanely demanding job at Mont-
clair State followed by two adjunct years at Amherst followed
by the unexpected invitation from Columbia, which is tenure-
track but which she intends to leave before they have the
chance to deny her tenure. She is, has always been, a traveler,
though Odin has revoked her visa. She can't raise him here, in
this cheaply furnished one-bedroom, and soon he'll be old
enough to mind about the condition of his house. The next
stop will, by definition, be more permanent.

   She's ready for that. She hopes she's ready.

Her students don't need to know about her current circumstances, especially not while they're so helplessly visible in their childhood bedrooms. There's an appalling intimacy now, coupled with a hollowed-out, unbroachable remove. The students are humbled by their own possessions. Last year, as autonomous figures on campus, they'd been their own manifestations, ragged or regal young warriors from faraway lands, whether they grew up in double-wides or suburban villas. They're more pitiful, beaming from the homes that have reeled them in again. They're more heartbreakingly earthbound, less interesting, less interested. If it's possible, at times, for Chess to feel like she's a droning, grade-B television show they're forced to watch, it's possible as well for her to feel less scorned and loved, less locked into the various entanglements of ire, impatience, and reverence she felt for them when they were in classrooms together. Now they've been revealed as the children they've always been.

Disembodied like this, Chess finds that she cares about them in a vaguely uncaring way. They are not her genuine concern. They are speaking to her (when they speak at all) not only from their own pasts but from their ongoing lives. It's never been more apparent that Chess doesn't matter, not deeply or lastingly, not when she's heard their dogs whining to be let in, their mothers walking into their rooms with freshly laundered towels, the ongoing lives in which Chess and all of Columbia are not much more than interruptions.

And besides, Chess truly cares only about Odin. Odin who, at seventeen months, is easily amused, whose greatest pleasures are opening and closing the doors of the kitchen cabinets or throwing his toys across the room so that Chess can retrieve them, when she's got the patience for it, so he can throw them again. He's especially fond of throw-and-retrieve with the lurid blue stuffed rabbit Garth gave him. Although Odin can't possibly know that that toy came from Garth, Chess can't help wondering how it is that this indifferently made thing, with its sewn-on black-dot eyes and the red round O of its mouth (thank you, Garth, for knowing about choking hazards), seems to win out over all the others—the crocheted elephant in the green vest, the shockingly expensive Steiff bear, all the toys in which Odin expresses only mild and cordial interest, as if they were awkward, unglamorous guests at a party.

It isn't bad, being cocooned like this, self-reliant, a tiny nation whose sole population is mother and child. She worries less. She's been assured by the Internet that a diet composed largely of Cheerios and cheese, the only food Odin considers to be food at all, will do him no lasting harm. In a different era, Chess would grow wearier sooner of the endless game of toss-and-retrieve, the opening and closing of the kitchen cupboards, Odin's unslakable desire to climb up onto the sofa, which is undiminished by his inability to do so; his new habit of pointing at objects of all kinds, to which Chess answers "lamp" or "chair" or "book" and sometimes, when he seems to be pointing at nothing in particular, "air" or "here" or "us." In their sequestered world, it's how the days pass. She is, in a way, seventeen months old, along with Odin. She's able to share his attachment to repetition, which resembles the chants of monks and nuns, reciting their devotions so unvaryingly that devotion becomes an involuntary bodily function, like breath and heartbeat.

Odin has yet to repeat most of the words Chess endeavors to

teach him. He has yet to mouth "lamp" or "chair," never mind "air" or "here." But when he walks unsteadily to the front window (he falls constantly, but unless he bumps his head, he doesn't mind about falling; it's another bead on the rosary, *throw open fall stand up again throw open fall*), he looks out through the glass and says "bird" (*brrrt*) or "car" (*kkar*), which are his only words at present, and which do not necessarily require the sighting of a bird or a car. He can look out at the street when there's no traffic, at the sky when it's empty of birds, and still invoke their names. He lives in a realm where the fantastic intersects with the real, where the two forces are still negotiating their way into a more orderly but less implausible and hallucinatory world. It won't last much longer. But for now the world remains an elaborate creation of Odin's, with its birds and cars, the empty air he points toward occasionally, seeking (or so Chess likes to think) an explanation not only for tables and lamps but for ether and emptiness as well. If he weeps sometimes in frustration or impatience or merely because happiness has suddenly and unpredictably abandoned him, he returns, always, to a condition of astonishment. Odin can remain long at the window, clutching the sill with both hands, gazing out with an expression of stunned rapture, as if he were looking onto a fictive and hypothetical place, a mythic realm he's invited to watch but that, unlike the rooms and their contents, he'll never be able to touch.

Chess's phone buzzes. Voice mail. She knows all too well who's calling.

Wolfe_man

Image: A slope of luminously green grass bisected by a trail of black earth. The trail leads up over the grassy hill to another, steeper hill and, eventually—though the trail itself vanishes—toward the purpled base of a faraway mountain. On the photograph's far left is the barely discernible stripe of a waterfall, a cataract tumbling down a rock face. The waterfall would be the object of most photographs but is, in this one, an incidental phenomenon, like the hint of a bystander inadvertently caught on film by someone taking a photograph of someone else. Robbie's sole object when he took the photo was the swell of grass with its line of trail, which cuts across the hill as precisely as the stroke of a knife.

Caption: We hike for about 5 miles and we can only hope we were right to trust the woman who rented the cabin to us, she wears her hair in one long gray braid which we both agree seems like a sign of honesty. Going off grid for a couple of days, will report back.

Robbie posted it five days ago. There's been nothing since.

Sitting on the stairs, Isabel times herself. She'll stare at the image for ten seconds. She's seen it dozens of times already. She's doing her best not to be a person of frightening intensity.

It's time for her to go back into the apartment. As a relatively normal person would.

When she enters the living room, she sees a note on the coffee table. The note wasn't there half an hour ago.

> Dear Mom and Dad please close the windows. Please remember. The kitchen was open. Please remember. Lovexxxx Violet

Dan enters from the bedroom, glassy-eyed. He's been composing.

Isabel says, "Did you see this?"

Dan frowns over the note. He's trying to remember how a concerned father would react.

"We should talk to her, right?" he says.

Yes, *we* should talk to her. Or *you* should talk to her, you *could* talk to her, will there ever be a time when the mother isn't expected to run the show?

If that time is coming, it won't be soon. What point, then, in arguing about which of them ought to shoulder this one? Especially when, if the fight goes badly, Isabel and Dan could only retreat to opposite ends of the apartment. Isabel could go back out onto the stairs again, though she's temporarily used up what she suspects is her allowance of on-the-stairs time before she becomes an object of Dan's increased concern, before he starts in, again, about the possibility of medication.

She says, "What exactly do we think it'll do, talking to her about this *again*?"

"Maybe we'll finally get through to her."

"Or we could just keep the windows closed."

"Well, yeah. But having some air circulation is nice, right?"

"It is. But picture being Violet. Picture being convinced that it blows in through every possible opening. Can you picture that?"

"Yeah. Sure I can. But is it a good idea to let her go on being afraid of something harmless like an open window?"

"She's six. Things like this pass away by themselves."

"Thank you, Doctor."

Thank *you,* Dan. Thank you for saying to me, *We should talk to her,* and mocking me when I give you an answer.

She says, "If you want to leave the windows open and talk her down from it, go ahead."

"No need to get testy."

"If you don't want to know what I have to say, don't ask."

Dan delivers one of his defeated shrugs. Isabel has been subject to that gesture for as long as she's known him. He's tried and failed. The forces arrayed against him are too powerful. He's stalwart and well-intentioned, but he knows, he knows all too well, when it's time to give in.

He says, "I'm gonna go back into the bedroom. I'm working on a new song."

"I've got about a hundred work emails."

"They never let up, do they?"

"They do not."

Dan delivers a kiss in her general direction and heads back to the bedroom. Isabel watches his retreating form, struggling to muster more affection for him, which, she's found, can be easier when he's leaving a room, not so much because he's removing himself but because it's more possible, then, to fully apprehend the fact that in leaving her he's entering another room where he'll be alone again with his music and his invisible followers, the isolated inhabitedness of his days. It matters that she empathizes with him, that she threads her way among the resentment, pity, and, worst, indifference that crowd and jostle her here, in these rooms, which, it seems, she will never leave again.

Nathan Walker-Byrne
Today 12:45 PM

Droogies you can come over tonight after 11 if you can get out of ur houses Ill leave the street door unlocked be QUIET when you come up to my place u were too loud last night Chad bring the tarot deck Harrison bring the gummys if you still have any stoner pig that you r but come over again OK im getting too used to my own stink so bring ur BO I swear ill smell ur pits like theyre roses ☺

sabel should go to the children, both of them, since Dan is unwilling, or unable. She should comfort Violet, which will entail another lecture from Violet about the ways in which Isabel needs to be more careful. She should engage again in the ongoing battle with Nathan, the grinding day-to-day between them, Isabel the empress who demands that Nathan, her captive, perform meaningless tasks (his homework, bathing) until his spirit has been imprisoned along with his body, until he agrees to spend his days digging holes and filling them back in again.

Then she should answer those emails.

She returns to the stairs. She takes her phone out of her pocket but forces herself not to look again at Robbie's Instagram posts. She dials up the Brahms *Requiem* instead. Yes, the *Requiem* is probably her own version of Violet's window closing, of Nathan's endless re-viewings of *School of Rock*. She gets that. She has not entirely taken leave of her senses. Not yet.

Mother needs a little something, too. She can't be counted on, not every minute of every day. She puts her earbuds into her ears. Even that gesture is consoling—the easy high-tech fit of them, the already-deepened quiet they bring even before she plays the Brahms. She hits Play, closes her eyes as the stringed instruments launch into the opening strains, that slow rising with its intimations of an anticipatory patience—*Hush, child, the story is beginning*—soon joined by the chorus, which, at this point, could almost be the voices of the instruments themselves, granted not only their own mournfully articulate swells and reverberations, their vocabularies of chords, but a muted solemn human language, as well.

To: Garth Byrne
Subject: Re:
From: Chess Mullins

Garth,

I've been cruel. Silence is the worst. I know that.

I've been in a nest of sorts with Odin, in what I'll call deep seclusion. I haven't been able to talk to anyone except my students, who are inescapable.

But otherwise I've been alone with Odin, and don't seem to have been able to communicate with anyone but him. This email is my first response to any living person who isn't a baby or an anxious undergraduate.

I'm sorry to say I don't think it's a good idea for you to touch him. Even if you've been in quarantine. Please don't gargle with bleach. I know that was a joke. But still.

I hope you can appreciate this. I can't let anyone near him but me.

I hope this isn't too melodramatic. But if you want to you could come over, stand on the sidewalk, and I'll bring him to the window. That might be a reference to some Greek play, but if it is I don't have the wherewithal to think of it.

Let me know. Outside of my classes, he and I are available pretty much anytime, any day.
Chess

From: Garth Byrne
Subject: Re:
To: Chess Mullins

Thank you. I can be there in about half an hour. I'll text when I get to your block. Thank you.

Violet sits expectantly on her bed, on the edge of the mattress, her feet planted on the floor. Someone will come and speak consolingly to her about how the kitchen window was carelessly opened, that the thing probably didn't get in, and that no window will ever be opened again. Somebody, her mother or father, will come soon, and tell her that. All she has to do is wait.

While she's waiting, she writes a letter.

> Hello Robbie this is a letter from Violet. Im doing spelling at school. The letters get together and dance. M is the queen letter. She is the prettiest. There's a bad letter that I'm not riting down at all. M is good. M is yello. I have on my yello dress. I like having it on in the day. I look like a star all the time. Mom is mad about the dress. Thank you for not being mad at me. I am going to look like a star the day you come home. See you soon. Love XXXXX Violet

The choir has progressed from its initial murmuring to one of the most fervent interludes, twenty minutes in. The hushed lullaby has swelled to ecstatic lament, an urgency as much like weather as it is like music, possessed of weather's inevitability, forceful but not emotional, not specifically emotional, more of the gathering storm than the merely human.

It's better that Isabel doesn't understand German. She prefers it this way. She's free to conceive a celebration of mortality itself, death as a beginning as well as an end, the cracking open of a glory that defies description but, when it reveals itself, may not be the cherubim and seraphim of the official glory Isabel was asked to aspire to as a girl, the painted clouds and winged children on the walls of Our Lady of Fatima. This is glory of another sort, a depthless luminous darkness or the wheel of a galaxy or a fire that cleanses as it burns everything away.

She listens to other music as well, everything from Beethoven to Radiohead, but she comes back, always, to the Brahms, which seems to affect her in the way of a lost mother, returned; a mother who sings to her about the terrors and splendors of the world; who's been far abroad and has come home, finally, to tell her daughter everything she's learned.

The first of the soloists is about to deliver his private lament. The chorus and the orchestra continue, but now, as the singer prepares to intone the opening notes, the loss is unutterably personal. Mortality fells everyone, but here is a lone man with a song of his own to sing.

Isabel should not be hiding out with Brahms like this. She's neglecting her children and her job. She'll get up soon and undertake her obligations. But she can't stop listening to the *Requiem,* not yet, not when the soloist is about to begin.

Iceland

April 5 2020

1. In the mornings when you open the window there's
this rush of a smell I can only call Green, it's not different
from the way the outdoors smells all the time but it's
stronger when the sun rises, it's like the smell of the wak-
ening world, and you're more aware of its components.
Roughly speaking: damp grass, some hint of iron that
must come from the rocks, plus what I can only think of
as old ice, a frozen kind of brisk non-smell, an underlayer
of cold. Cold it seems is always here, cold is the true condition it only goes underground in spring and summer
but it's always there and it pushes the spring smells that
much more to the surface, it's like the plant life sort of
skates over the ice for a while. It's really strong in the
mornings.

2. The landscape in early April is still spare. There are
according to the book I bought in Reykjavik some flowers
still to come later in the season with names like Lupine
and sheep sorrel and Arctic thyme but now it's all grass
and moss and a hardy small white flower called the
mountain avens, just a circle of white petals, they look

like those dancing flowers in the old cartoons that scared us when we were kids. The guidebook says, I quote, in Icelandic folklore the flower is allegedly imbued with the power to attract wealth, but first, you must steal money from an impoverished widow while she is attending church and then bury the spoils underneath a spot where the flower grows. The legend goes that your ill-gotten gains will then double.

Needless to say we really love this book.

3. Wolfe was here earlier but he's gone, I'm sure he said he was going for a hike. He's quiet and quixotic (points for using "quixotic" in a sentence). He doesn't exactly live in time. I don't mind that he's imaginary but I lose track sometimes of the fact that he is.

4. There's a holiness here. A nearness to something.

5. There's a bookshelf over the bed and a fox skull, very clean and white, nailed to the wall beside the shelf, as if the books and the skull were somehow related. Aunt Zara hung a crucifix over her bed but as far as I remember she didn't have any books. The crucifix fascinated me when I was a kid, this tiny wooden man mostly naked with his arms spread, up there on Aunt Zara's wall. Aunt Zara's Christ was one of the hunky ones with abs and shoulders as opposed to the gaunt skeletal ones. Zara was the most Catholic person in our family but she liked her Salems and her vodka stingers along with her hot muscular Christ and she believed in expensive shoes. Aunt Zara is in some heaven that wouldn't be at all like Iceland but I feel confident is the right heaven for her, probably more like Palm Springs.

Here ends today's entry, written in a composition note-book produced by the Mead Company, made somewhere in India, purchased from the Staples in Union Square and conveyed to a place where if it weren't for this cabin it could seem as if no one not one single human being has ever been before.

I remain yours, I remain mine, I remain watchful and largely unimaginary, Robert Q Walker

Garth Byrne
Today 2:10 PM

OMG. Hes a MAN. Hes our man. Im not even a block
away but i had to text u right away it was SO AMAZING
to see him growing up u looked good too even tho I know
you never sleep ok im having a reaction about me having
just been some guy out there on the street waving to him
i had this idea for a second that he recognized me but
that's my narcissism speaking ive been working on the
idea that there are other people in the world ☺ THANK
YOU for this i hope we can do it again soon xxxooo

sabel, out on the stairs, has received a text from Dan, just as the Brahms is reaching its crescendo.

Dan Byrne
Today 2:34 PM
R u ok out there?

Isabel Walker
Today 2:34 PM
Where are you?

Today 2:34 PM
Living room

Today 2:35 PM
Why are u texting me?

Today 2:35 PM
Can I come out?

Today 2:35 PM
I'll come to u.

She finds Dan sitting in what strikes her as the exact middle of the sofa, as if he's measured it. That can't be true. He does, however, sit with an air of formality, as if he were waiting for a train in a crowded station.

"Why would you text me?" she asks.

"I try to leave you alone when you're out there."

"Mm-hm."

"So I texted you instead."

"What's up?"

"The kids are in their rooms."

"It's school. Not that we think Nathan really *is* in school at the moment, I have to go check up on him—"

Dan says, "When we found Violet's note. We had kind of a fight, didn't we?"

"I don't know if I'd call it a fight."

"Maybe that's the thing. We couldn't really fight. We *can't* really fight. The kids will hear us."

"Do you think we need to fight?"

"I've been thinking about this morning."

"It wasn't that big a deal."

"It felt like a big deal. To me. Even if it didn't look that way. I felt like I was, I don't know. Falling away. From you and the kids and everything."

"You got emotional when Nathan called you an asshole. Why wouldn't you get emotional about that?"

"I should go talk to him."

"I already did."

"But I should, too. I don't know why I haven't, yet."

"If you're worried about interrupting his *studies*—"

"This morning I was . . . I don't know. Afraid of him. How weird is that? Our little boy."

Dan has grown denser over time. He's not fat, but neither is he athletically graceful anymore. He's taken on a weighted quality, as if he moves through his own atmosphere of slightly heavier air. She wonders if it's time to tell him to stop bleaching his hair.

Dan says, "When Nathan called me that—"

"He didn't mean it."

"Sure he meant it. I meant it when I called *my* father an asshole."

"But in the bigger picture—"

"He asked me to stop singing. I kept singing. I thought I was this chipper dude with a song in his heart. Like, some kind of *Can't Stop the Music* shit."

"You were only singing one of your songs."

"Yeah, well, my songs. It's okay that you don't really like them."

"I've told you I do. Over and over."

"Maybe it's the over and over that tips me off. What do we think when somebody says they've told us something *over and over*?"

"Please don't get like this."

When did Dan's defeats and, worse, his victories, become more unbearable to her than her own?

"The songs aren't really for you," he says. "They're for Robbie."

"Dan, I'm tired," she says. "I can't really have this conversation."

"I mean they're *for* Robbie."

"I'm not really sure what it is you're talking about."

"I seem to want Robbie to know that I'm not nobody."

"Nobody thinks you're nobody."

"Nathan does."

"Nathan is eleven."

"I wish Robbie would come back."

"He will. Whenever he can."

"Iceland."

"Iceland."

Dan says, "Robbie isn't attractive to me. Okay, he's not *not* attractive, but you know what I mean. He knows how I feel about him. Which means he can listen to the songs and not think, *This is about me*. Beyond lust there's a purity, you know?"

"I'm honestly not sure what you're getting at."

"I was this . . . pretty boy. I know that's a funny thing to say about myself. But. How were you not going to marry some twenty-year-old dude who was your little brother's new best friend?"

"This is so not true."

A silence passes.

Dan says, "Do you think chicken or fish for dinner tonight?"

"Either."

"We should have the fish. It's been in the freezer awhile."

"Okay."

"Can I tell you something funny?"

"Yes."

"I think my father started to drift away after my mother started asking him at breakfast what he thought he wanted for dinner. Guess what. I was always so afraid I was turning into my father I forgot to watch out for, you know, the other thing."

She sits beside him on the sofa. They could be waiting for the same train. She puts an arm over his shoulders and, when he doesn't react, takes her arm away again.

She says, "When we're not . . . like this . . ."

"We don't know when that will be."

"It won't be forever."

"But whenever it changes, it won't make that much difference, will it?"

"I don't know."

"I thought if I was a musician again, it would change things."

"Dan, sweetheart—"

"You've tried so hard to be in love with me."

She has no idea how to respond to that.

Does it ever get to be *too late*? If neither of you abuses the
dog (should they finally get a dog?) or leaves the children in the
car on a hot day. Does it ever become irreparable? If so, when?
How do you, how does anyone, know when they cross over
from *working through this* to *it's too late*? Is there (she suspects
there must be) an interlude during which you're so bored or
disappointed or ambushed by regret that it is, truly, too late?
Or, more to the point, do we arrive at *it's too late* over and over
again, only to return to *working through this* before *it's too late*
arrives, yet again?

She says, "We should wait. We should just be patient, and
wait. Don't you think?"

"I do. Sure I do. I think I'm going to make the chicken instead of the haddock tonight."

"Whatever."

"I feel like the haddock's been in the freezer too long. We
should probably just throw it out."

"Chicken would be fine."

"I agree. Chicken would be fine."

G arth had never intended to be a man standing on a sidewalk waving with slightly desperate vigor (*Hey, look over here!*) to a child in a window. He'd never intended to be a desperately waving man, someone the child doesn't recognize.

He'd never intended to fall in love with Chess.

When did that happen? How did that happen?

Garth stomps down Bergen Street. Odin is so changed that Garth might not have recognized him if—will Chess deign to admit it?—he weren't growing to look ever more like her. Even in a kid this young, here's Chess's broad and stately face, here are her wide-set gray eyes. Here, in a toddler.

Chess has grown handsomer. She's more like sculpture, white marble with that ancient Greek expression of what Garth can only call serene ferocity. Or maybe it's because he hasn't seen her in so long. Maybe he's lost track of her unorthodox beauty, the ways in which her face is not exactly contemporary. It's not hard to picture her at dusk during harvest season, with a sheaf of wheat under one arm and a lamb under the other.

She did not smile at him as he stood waving from the sidewalk. She nodded. It was less than he'd hoped for, but Chess has never been much of a smiler. She's of the opinion (she told him so, years ago, when they were living in the dump on Water

Street) that it's best if a woman refrains from smiling too much, and from any other indication of a desire to please.

Odin merely stared at Garth, uncomprehendingly. Why was he being asked to look at this stranger? Another woman, a different kind of mother, might have raised one of Odin's hands in a simulated wave. Chess is not that kind of mother.

April 5, 2020

Dear Isabel,

Let's see if I still know how to write. Let's see if the ink in this pen doesn't run out, it's the only pen I've got. I forgot to pack a pen, I never really thought of writing as opposed to texting until we got here. I did pack two pairs of uncomfortable shoes and a fancy shirt for some European party I'd never get invited to. No pen, though.

But do you know they sell Bic pens everywhere? Even in Reykjavik.

It's funny, ~~isn't it~~, when some incidental thing like a pen reveals itself as some kind of precious object. If I hadn't happened to buy this pen at the airport, I'd be completely unable to write anything at all, given that I'm about 30 miles from the nearest place that might sell pens. Can't help thinking about an apocalyptic future when we're huddled together remembering how we used to just stop into a store and buy a pen, or a lighter or a roll of toilet paper.

I have no idea when I'll be able to send this, it won't be from here. I will have been able to call you long before you get this. This is like a message in a bottle, tossed into the ocean, to be washed up on some future shore.

But I want to talk to you, even if it's in a letter you may not get for weeks. Bic pens don't really run out of ink, do they? Which would account for their global popularity.

Enough about the pen. Where to begin?

We're way up in the mountains. You have to hike to it, there's no road, only a trail.

It's almost ridiculously beautiful. This one-room house in the middle of a field on the side of a mountain that, even as mountains go, is impressive. I can hear the sound of the waterfall nearby, which is ~~tumbling~~ flowing down from, yes, the glacier on top of the mountain. From one of the two tiny windows—there's a notable lack of windows in spite of the view—we can see down to the plain way way below. The mountains are covered with grass but the plain, being volcanic, is all black rock, with outcroppings of neon-green moss and thermal pools the color of swimming pools at night. That insanely vivid aqua color.

We walk around naked when it's warm enough, which is mostly for a few hours around noon. Add Walking Naked on a Mountain in Iceland to your to-do list. Under the general category heading Go to Iceland.

I wonder if any of those med school letters have arrived yet. I know I'm a bit of a long shot, what with my shall we say unorthodox background, but I'm choosing to think they'll offer at least a few spots to the unorthodox, ergo someone like me. And I only need to be accepted by one of them.

Being away like this has helped me feel that much better about my new life. I want a new life for you too, but that, I suspect, is another subject for another letter. Anyway, I think I could heal people. I'd like to try.

And you know I do have hope. ~~Why not have hope?~~ I love the new future, assuming we survive the present. And assuming we survive the present in some form or other we're going to need more doctors, more than ever.

I've got a copy of Mill on the Floss here. They had entered the thorny wilderness, and the golden gates of their childhood had for ever closed behind them. How much do we love George Eliot?

Do you think we ever really survive our childhoods?

Love,
Robbie

After Garth has performed his wave-and-dance routine and moved on, Chess and Odin are restored to their private world. Garth's presence, fleeting and remote as it was, has proven to be a bigger incursion than she'd expected it to be.

And now, here's Garth's text. *OMG. Hes a MAN. Hes our man.* Et cetera.

Odin takes up the blue rabbit but does not throw it. He merely holds it at arm's length, scrutinizes it, as if it were . . . not new, but newly revealed to him as a parallel twin of the familiar rabbit.

Odin can't associate the rabbit with Garth. That's not possible.

Class begins in less than an hour. It's time to start getting Odin ready for his nap, which requires a prelude of Let's Quiet Down Now. But first, there's something Chess has to do.

Back in the bedroom—where else is there for him to go?—Dan is starting on a new song. What else is there for him to do, now that the question of dinner has been decided?

We never thought of curses and spells
We didn't know about all the hells
No good. Start over.

Nathan starts *School of Rock* again. Here's Jack, stripping off his shirt onstage, diving into a crowd that doesn't catch him, lying facedown on the floor. As Nathan watches, he texts:

Nathan Walker-Byrne
Today 3:00 PM

PS boyz I am so gonna lead us to victory at Legends cuz I've only been playing it and jerking off Im now a TOTAL GOD at both just so obey me when I speak see u tonight just BE QUIET OK? There are hidden microphones around here.

Violet, in her bedroom, begins to realize that no one is coming to reassure her. She goes to the mirror in her yellow dress, to remind herself about how pretty she is, wearing it.

Her mother appears behind her, reflected in the mirror.

Violet says, "Did you see my note?" She speaks to her mother's reflection.

"Mm-hm."

"Be more careful, okay?"

"Honey—"

A cloudiness rises in her mother's face. She is an obvious person. Violet herself is more mysterious, better possessed of what she's recently learned to call *bearing*. Violet is practiced, already, at appearing to be calm and self-possessed, like Sara in *A Little Princess*.

Violet's mother says, "I think the blue dress is my favorite."

"You don't like this one?"

"I like all your dresses. I just think you look really nice in the blue."

"This one is my favorite."

"It's a very pretty dress. But yellow can be . . . hard to wear."

Violet's mother doesn't always make sense. Violet continues speaking to her mother's reflection. "It still *fits*," she says.

"I didn't mean it's hard to put the dress *on*. I meant . . . Never mind. Wear the yellow dress. Wear anything you want."

"You don't like this dress," Violet says.

"I love it. I love everything you do. The windows are all closed. We're having chicken tonight. Not fish."

"Okay."

"And really, you're right about everything. Don't ever let me or anybody else argue with you, ever. About anything."

A second later, her mother's reflection vanishes. Violet is alone in the mirror again. It seems possible that a different mother lives inside the mirror, nearly identical to her real mother but older and angrier. The mirror mother might be her mother's future self, invisible when you look at her directly but revealed by the truth of the mirror. When Violet's own reflection performs a half-turn, the mirror offers back a pretty girl in a dress that floats and shimmers, a dress the color of sunlight, a dress chosen for her by Robbie, who, when he comes back, will want to see her in it. Robbie does not envy Violet, he does not want her to doubt herself or to feel diminished or to question her increasing awareness of herself as well-favored, gifted and graceful, the girl in a story about a girl like her. Robbie will be back soon, and when he's back, the world will not only make more sense, it'll be more thoroughly infused with jokes and hope, with the sparkling bounty, the bigheartedness, Robbie took with him when he went away.

From: Chess Mullins
Subject: Re:
To: Garth Byrne

Garth,

I'm glad you got to see Odin, and that you were so moved by seeing him.

I have to tell you, though, that I'm disconcerted by the phrase "our man." He is not our man. He is a baby. He is my baby. You are not one of his parents. I am his parent.

We agreed that Odin should know you. We were clear about that. But that was, and is, as far as it goes. I have the impression, from your text, that you've begun to think of us as some kind of couple, which we are not. I do want Odin to know the man whose genes he carries. But I do not want him to feel confused about having any kind of traditional mother and father.

It was odd, more than I'd expected it to be, to stand in the window holding Odin while you smiled and waved up at him from the street. I'm sure it wasn't easy for you, either, whatever you said in your text. I felt like there was something ever so slightly archetypal about it, a woman holding a child for a man to see, from behind glass.

We need to think about our boundaries. It might be best for you to take some time away. From Odin and from me. I don't think I can give you what you seem to want. I'm sorry. I hope you believe that.

Chess

"Hello?"

"Hi, Dad."

"Isabel, hello there. It's been a while."

"I called the day before yesterday."

"Did you? The days are so. You lose track, you know."

"I do."

"Are you all right? Are Dan and the kids all right?"

"Yes. Relatively speaking. I wanted to make sure *you're* all right."

"I'm fine, honey. I poached myself an egg, for lunch."

"That sounds nice."

"Your mother would never have allowed it. Eggs for lunch. Downfall of civilization."

"I've been thinking about Mom."

"It's a shame we can't go see her. I hate to think about what's left of the flowers we took, last time."

"Tulips. They were tulips."

"They'd just be stems, by now."

"Dad."

"Yes, honey?"

"I've been thinking about Mom."

"You and me both."

"I don't mean I *don't* think about her all the time. But I've been wondering if you think she was happy. I know that's a slightly impossible question."

"She wouldn't be happy about the tulips, I can tell you that. Just a vase full of stems."

"I was so hard on her."

"You were spirited. Like your mother. Do you know she refused to marry me because I wasn't much of a dancer?"

"I know, I've heard that one. It's a funny story. But lately I've been thinking about some of those fights she and I had."

"I wasn't Catholic and I couldn't dance. Two strikes against me."

"Yes. And she married you anyway. It's a great story."

"I'm a pretty determined kind of guy."

"You are."

"So I signed up for lessons at the Arthur Murray Dance Academy. And I converted. It wasn't like being a Seventh-day Adventist mattered to me, one way or the other."

"Have you been going to mass? I'm sure you can Zoom something like that."

"Honey, mass was your mother's thing. I just sort of tagged along with her until, you know . . ."

"I'm glad our house wasn't all full of crucifixes and statues of saints and things."

"Your mother wasn't that kind of person. Our house always looked pretty normal, right?"

"It did. It looked very normal."

"Your mother did want you and your brother to go to mass, though. She didn't really mind about my eternal soul. She was much more worried about you and Robbie."

"She and I had some fights about that. Along with everything else."

"Mothers and daughters have their differences."

"I feel like I was really awful, though. I said terrible things."

"I'm sure she took it all in stride."

"But you don't *know* if she did."

"We didn't talk much about all that. By bedtime, we were too tired. We worked hard, back then."

"I know. You both worked very hard, I know that."

"And you think you'll have some of those conversations later. When there's more time."

"I tried to get back home."

"There's nothing you can do if you're stuck at an airport, is there?"

"Robbie, too."

"He was on his way. You were both on your way. They didn't tell us it could happen that quickly. They should tell you things like that."

"I guess they don't really know. I'm pretty sure they told us. That it was going to be hard to predict."

"Remember that young doctor? Green, I think his name was Green. Or Rose. A color. Could it have been Dr. Rose?"

"I think his name was Greenblatt. Dad, I shouldn't be bothering you with this."

"You're not bothering me. It's always good to hear from you."

"Do you have everything you need?"

"Me? Sure. Nina leaves the groceries out front."

"And you disinfect everything."

"What I'd like is to replace your mother's flowers."

"There aren't any florists open."

"Get rid of the stems, then. I don't like it, a vase full of old flower stems."

"I'll see what I can do."

"You're a good girl. You and Robbie are both good kids. What have you heard from Robbie?"

"He's still in Iceland."

"I know."

"I'm slightly worried about him."

"As far as I know, Iceland isn't a very dangerous country."

"Every place seems dangerous, don't you think?"

"I hear Iceland is pretty safe. I do keep up on the news, you know."

"I know."

"Iceland. We thought it was a big deal going to Fort Lauderdale in the summers."

"I think I can go to the cemetery and get rid of the old flowers."

"I'd appreciate that. Your mother would, too."

"It's funny. I want to take back some of the things I said to Mom, years ago, and you want to get rid of those dead flowers."

"Sorry, I couldn't hear that. Another ambulance went by. Those sirens are so loud."

"I was trying to say something about Mom."

"She always said I was the son of a gun who danced his way into her heart."

"Did she say anything? About me. At, you know, the end. I'm sorry I keep asking that."

"She was medicated. Dr. Green said it was best."

"As opposed to being in pain."

"I was there. And Zara. And that nice nurse, I forget her name."

"Lavinia. The nurse's name was Lavinia."

"Right. Lavinia. African American girl. Young Dr. Green could have taken a lesson from her, about how to talk to patients."

"So Mom didn't really say much of anything. She was too out of it."

"She slipped away very peacefully. I do hope Dr. Green didn't give her slightly too much, but we didn't want her to be in any pain, did we?"

"I can go to the cemetery and get rid of the dead flowers. I can do that."

"Thank you. Be careful, though."

"I will. I'll call you tomorrow."

"That'd be nice."

April 5, 2020

Dear Violet, 15 Years from Now,

I never thought I'd write one of these. A letter to your future self. I'm not really that kind of mother. I'm not really that kind of person.

But as it turns out I am writing it because I suspect I'll never do it when the times become less strange again.

Full disclosure. There will be no revelation about a secret inheritance or, really, about a secret of any kind. I don't want to set you up for something I'm not going to deliver.

It's this.

Since we've been locked up together, I've seen you in ways I never had before and probably never will again. Because we've had, God knows, plenty of alone time.

I've been irritated by you twice already, today. And I've been cold to you, I've done that mother thing: Fine Just Do Whatever You Want I Don't Care, that thing, which is (trust me) one of a mother's only ways of fighting back.

As a mother you have almost nothing to fight back with when you're dealing with a six-year-old. You use whatever you've got because your child has no mercy,

your child doesn't care about your feelings, your child is
free to hate you and tell you about it, in detail. Which is as
it should be.

That said, who wants to be told that you're letting
something deadly in because you leave a window open
and then go on from that to how you've gotten so fat your
child doesn't want to look at you anymore? You were
probably right about that, not the window being open but
me getting fat (it's only maybe eight pounds), but anyway.
You can say it. You're completely allowed to say it. You're
completely allowed to look hatefully at me while you tell
me you can't look at me anymore.

Actually it's probably more like ten pounds. I've
stopped weighing myself. I know I wasn't exactly gra-
cious when you said you couldn't look at me anymore. I
can't really look at myself anymore, either.

And so the only counterattack for the fat old mother
who really isn't enthusiastic about hearing the truth is to
say, Fine, then. No more love, no more bedtime stories,
and I guess you'll be buying your own clothes from
now on.

My mother did it to me. I'm still getting over my shock
that I do it to you. I'd like to think you won't do it to your
own child IF you decide you want to have one, which you
DON'T HAVE TO, no matter what anybody may tell
you.

I want to be sure you know you're not wrong about
this. I love you, probably more than I ever thought I could
love anyone, but please don't let anybody convince you
that you've made up stories about a mother who could go

suddenly cold and distant on you. You haven't made those stories up.

A mother is not innocent. She can't be. Too much is asked of her. Don't let a therapist talk you into owning too much of your own responsibility.

I know how strange it is to say things like this. But I think you might as well know. And I suppose I'm also saying it so you'll trust what I'm going to say next.

You're an extraordinary person.

Which is not just maternal sentimentality speaking. Most mothers think their children are amazing and singular people. Most mothers are wrong about that. How many amazing, singular people do you know, whatever their mothers think of them?

In your case, it's true. About being extraordinary. I honestly might have missed it in you if everything were normal, if it was all about me getting to work on time, myself, while getting you to school and making playdates with your friends, which got more complicated after Uncle Robbie moved out and your father was working seriously on his music. Plus trying to talk you out of some truly mortifying outfits. Please use the canary-yellow frilly thing as an example of what you should NEVER EVER wear. I can't believe Uncle Robbie bought it for you—he of all people should know that white people should never wear yellow.

But anyway, that's mothers and daughters during normal times, right? We're running a business together, in a way. We're in the business of getting you to grow up at least relatively undamaged, we do everything we can to keep the business afloat. New clothes that respect your very early sense of style, three meals a day and never some microwaved garbage even though that's what you'd prefer, the ongoing effort to be firm but generous, etc. etc. etc. While retaining some shred of my own self-esteem. The business takes up so much of our time and attention that we don't exactly get to know each other.

Unless we're marooned together on the tiny planet known as our house. Which has given me the chance to see you in ways I probably wouldn't have, otherwise.

I've seen how patient you are with your brother and your father. Well, your father, no one expects a little girl to be patient with her older brother. But how many six-year-old girls, stuck at home when you should be starting out into the world, would be like you? How many six-year-olds in a situation like this think of others before they think of themselves?

For instance, this morning, when your father started crying after he and Nathan had that fight, you went over to him and stood beside him, you just stood there, like . . . what? His accomplice in that moment of crazy desolation, I suppose. You knew a hug would have been too much, it would have slightly mortified him. You just went and stood beside him. You knew to do that.

That's not all that much by way of an example, I don't really have a lot of examples—it's not as if you saved a baby from drowning or rescued us from a fire or anything like that. NOT that you need to have done anything like that, to be an extraordinary person. Mothers are probably doomed to a life of apology. That, too, is another subject for another time.

I'm not the best mother in the world, but I do have my share of what I'll call motherly ESP, which seems to come with the territory. I'm aware of your, what to call it? Precocious humanity. The depths of your being, if that's not too corny for you to bear.

Your father can really only focus on his music, along with keeping things going, day to day. Your brother lives upstairs. And I'm, I don't know, I'm here, but I can't seem to be all that helpful to anyone, you included. I guess I'm not really unreservedly HERE.

I hope, by the time you read this, that we're the kind of mother and daughter who can talk about whatever boy or girl you're dating, a mother and daughter who go to lunch together, and etc., but I have a feeling that's not going to be us. Don't get me wrong, I'd love that. But I have a feeling about it.

Does it sound ridiculous if I say that one of my greatest joys, currently one of my only joys, is knowing you? Just knowing you.

PS. By the time you read this, I'm sure Nathan and your father will be best friends. I hope it's not too hard on you, when they get into it like that. It's fathers and sons. It's REALLY fathers and sons when they're trapped together, 24/7.

PPS. I'm not sorry about the yellow dress. I'm sorry I was so mean about it. It seems you and I have had some fights lately, which is probably all too predictable between a mother and daughter. But I admit that I'm not very sorry about the dress itself. Yellow, as I may have mentioned, isn't really your color, yellow may not really be anyone's color, but it's one of those things only a mother will tell you.

You look great in everything else. Trust me about that,
too. You're beautiful in your own skin. You brought with
you into the world some kind of human amazingness,
and you can depend on it, always. Please try not to ever let
anybody talk you out of that.

Love,
Mom

Garth Byrne
Today 2:30 PM
I know we're not a couple I KNOW that but I'm still Odin's father OK

Chess Mullins
Today 2:31 PM
How to put this so it makes sense to you?

Today 2:31 PM
give it ur best shot

Today 2:32 PM
I asked you because we're friends and I thought you'd respect the boundaries. It's a funny thing to write in a text, I know.

Today 2:32 PM
Very funny

Today 2:33 PM
We should talk about this. I mean TALK about it.

Today 2:33 PM
Through a window?

Today 2:33 PM
No. We should wait until it feels less dangerous.

Today 2:34 PM
I could be dead by then

Today 2:34 PM
That's dramatic.

Today 2:34 PM
I feel dramatic right now

Today 2:35 PM
All right. To the best of my ability, on my phone keys. You're my friend. You're a gifted artist.

Today 2:35 PM
Thanks

Today 2:35 PM
And you have what I'll call a personal force. I'm sure you know what I mean.

Today 2:36 PM
I'm also tall w symmetrical features its a DNA thing right

Today 2:36 PM
It wasn't as coldhearted as that.

Today 2:36 PM
It could pass for coldhearted if u squint at it

Today 2:37 PM
This is an insane way for us to have this conversation.

Today 2:37 PM
Ill call u

Today 2:37 PM
Now?

"Hello, Garth."

"You picked up."

"I almost didn't."

"By ring number five I figured that out. What were you say-ing, about men with personal force and, you know, good DNA?"

"I was saying it wasn't as coldhearted as it probably sounds."

"It does kind of sound that way, you agree?"

"I don't want a man in my life. I've never wanted a man in my life."

"But."

"You know this. I didn't really like the idea of an anony-mous donor. You *know* this. We've talked about it."

"You've got a lot of faith in *We've talked about it.*"

"I have to take some responsibility."

"For what's going on."

"I think I brought you into Odin's life more than I should have."

"And hey, I was a lot cheaper than a babysitter."

"And *hey,* we'd agreed that he'd know you as he grew up. It's only that it got to be a bit . . . much."

"The plan was more like, would I drop off some diapers on my way home."

"Please don't oversimplify."

"Would I babysit for him on your teaching days. Back when there were teaching days."

"I said I take *some* responsibility. Did that sound to you like I was saying I'm some sort of scheming harridan who threw you under the bus when she didn't need you any longer?"

"I didn't mean that."

"I know you didn't. I know you're upset."

"I'm really upset."

"I know."

"I never thought I'd love the little fucker like this. Wait a minute. Do you think that was too much of a *man* thing to call him? Little fucker?"

"No. I call him that, too."

"Did I hear you laugh, just then?"

"My reputation as humorless and heartless is only partly true."

"I shouldn't say what I want to say."

"Maybe you shouldn't."

"But I see you in him, and then I see him in you. And it fucks with me. It breaks my heart, ever so slightly. I'm sorry."

"You don't need to apologize."

"What I guess I'm trying to say. I see this kind of *quality* in you and I see it in him."

"He's got all kinds of qualities, which, as far as I can tell, are his own."

"Okay. I see this, it's hard to know how to put it, this, like, *gravity* that's invisible in him and in you but I can feel it, I can see it, and what it feels like and looks like in the kid is the same as what it feels like and looks like in you. I mean, he's *ours*. I should probably stop talking, right?"

"You should definitely stop."

"Will you think about not shutting me out?"

"I'll think about it, yes."

"Can I at least come back and do another dance out on the sidewalk, for him?"

"I'll think about it."

"Great. Yes. Please think about it."

sabel descends the stairs and walks outside. The afternoon light, pallid and unwarming, seems to coalesce in the air rather than emanate from the sky, more like a wan, permeating glow than actual sun. There are no cars. There's no one on the sidewalk. The street, unpopulated, awash in sourceless light, could be a photograph of itself. Across the street the Shoe Hospital remains closed, its sign unlit. The reflection of the street itself skims over its front window. Behind the glass and what it reflects is the raccoon (or maybe it really is a fox), barely visible, still raising its cobbler's hammer, which never comes down. A siren blares, from several blocks away.

A minute passes, and another, before Isabel starts out. It's two and a half miles to the cemetery.

She's embarked on the most meaningless of errands: the removal of a dozen long-dead tulips from her mother's grave. It matters only to her father, who'd have no way of knowing otherwise if she just *told* him she'd done it.

Still, she's doing it.

She doubts that she'll linger at the grave. She and Robbie were both opposed to burial—they'd have preferred cremation, followed by scattering in the East River—but their father was adamant (*I can't have her burned up and thrown into the water*). Their father was, had to be, the deciding vote.

And so the search for a plot in Green-Wood, where prime

real estate is limited. And so casket shopping, headstone shopping (granite, marble, fieldstone), the debate over the inscription, which (outvoted again) is "Beloved Wife and Mother." If their father had agreed to cremation, Isabel and Robbie might have been spared their own three-martini jokes about the inscription, the night after the service (*She Wasn't All That Bad,* no, wait, *This Doesn't Mean You Can Start Fucking with Her Now*), followed by their morning-after embarrassment. They really had gone too far.

Although their mother doesn't care, she doesn't belong in a cemetery, a Beloved Wife and Mother.

Isabel will, however, walk the distance and get rid of the stems. She won't linger at the grave itself, but she doesn't mind the idea of a walk through the cemetery, among its spires and pyramids and obelisks, the angel with the scoured-away face (a favorite) seated with her lap full of eroded stone roses, the kind of angel Isabel could believe in if she believed in angels at all—entities in human form but innocent of identifiable human features. Isabel doesn't mind the idea of a walk through the cemetery, a necropolis with its chapels and palaces, heroes and angels along with its simple headstones, all those manifestations of the multitudes—celebrated and obscure alike—who, at least, are no longer worried about dying.

April 5, 2020

Dear Isabel,

Letter number two. I didn't say everything in today's first letter which by the way is sitting on the table waiting for the day when Wolfe and I return to civilization and find a post office. Along with a letter to the kids that I wrote earlier.

I think I should tell you. I feel kind of sick. I don't really feel up to walking back down. And Wolfe has gone for a hike.

I'm not worried, not really worried. ~~Why not have faith?~~ This cough I've got isn't exactly better but it's not any worse, either. I'm pretty tired, but what sick, nervous person isn't.

It would have been a good idea to bring along a carrier pigeon.

Speaking of birds there's a species of owl here that's not in the guidebooks. These owls are small, not much bigger than pigeons, and grayish-brown. They fly around, at night. The sky is full of them.

The nights are amazing. They're completely silent and dark or anyway the Earth is dark but the sky blazes away

with satellites and galaxies and spaceships not to mention
all those owls and some other winged animals which are
like bats but they're not bats, it's hard to say what they
are. They could be flying rabbits but they're not rabbits
either.

It's kind of frightening, I won't deny that. Who isn't
afraid of the night? I'm not sure how to put this but the
nights feel like this gigantic illuminated semidarkness you
could join, you could be part of.

There's this feeling that you don't need to keep the
night outside, here. That said it's hard to tell whether it's
a good idea to let the night in, either. There's this room
I'm in, the kerosene lamp is slightly harsh but effective
and . . . how to put this? Isn't there a fable about the
house vs. the woods, and they're both dangerous? I'm
probably making that up.

I'm glad I had the good sense to pack a copy of Mill on
the Floss. It's even better than I remembered. Please add
to your own personal check list, Read Mill on the Floss
again.

OK I'm a little nervous. I'm a little afraid. The letter to
Nathan and Violet of course doesn't say anything about,
you know, anything. I know you and Dan are great with
them but it's deeply weird, me not being there while all
this is going on.

I mean, how long should they go without the guiding
influence and spiritual uplift only their uncle can provide?

Joke. Obviously. I hope it's obvious.

Do you remember when I was six, and the Naumans'
dog bit me? The dog wasn't really to blame, I was being

too rough with it and really how much roughness can a toy
poodle be expected to feel OK about. But I was afraid of
dogs after that. I want to make a joke about myself being
traumatized by a toy poodle but I can't quite think of how
to put it. Please god don't take away my sense of humor.
Anyway I'm not sure exactly when it was, probably a year
later, you and I were walking to school and some guy was
coming toward us with a dog on a leash (beagle?) and I
was all set to run off in the other direction but you took me
by the hand and asked the guy if it was OK to pet the dog,
he said it was, and you put my trembling freaked-out hand
onto the dog's head. You whispered to me. I don't remember what you said it would have been reassurances but I
seem to remember it as music, like you were singing to me,
and I patted the dog's head and the dog wagged its tail and
everything was all right and I wasn't afraid of dogs anymore (run-on sentence, I wouldn't have tolerated this from
one of my sixth graders but you can't erase ink plus I may
not be quite totally in my right mind

I may not be. It's hard to tell. But I do want you to
know I have this really vivid memory of you singing to
me even though you were speaking to me while I patted a
beagle's head and wasn't afraid of dogs anymore.

I want to tell you I remember that.

I want to tell you this, too.

I'm scared, there's no denying it. I can't tell how sick I
am. But there's this too. I want to be sure you know about
this.

I don't think I've ever been so aware of the glory of the
world. Way up here where we see the same view all day

every day and there's no denying that it's one hell of a
view but I'm not going to try to describe it to you, I'm not
very good at that kind of thing. Grass, glacier, river,
sky—you know what to do with that information.

By the way it's not only the nights. The sky here sings,
during the days. You have to listen for it. It's not a joyful
voice, not exactly joyful. Remember when we were teen-
agers, that joke we had about how we didn't really want
to go to heaven if it meant wearing white robes and flying
around a chalice all the time? Spending eternity in a city
on fire seemed a lot more interesting? Maybe you were
the one who said that. You were a bad girl. Needless to
say I love you for that.

Anyway the sky when it sings in daytime is more like a
Gregorian chant than anything else, though that's not exactly right. It's some sort of musical rumble, it's deep and
I want to say sonorous but that's not quite right either. It's
reverent in its way but not supplicant, it's sort of like God
singing to herself . . .

Let's say that the sky here is an impossibly piercing
blue and it sings sometimes, and then night comes again
and the stars and satellites are out.

I feel like I'm getting this all wrong. And I'm not really
persuasively sure what I'm seeing and hearing as opposed to.

What I do want to try and say is that up here I feel time
passing through me, passing through the world, in ways I
never have before. It's always been event + event + event =
whatever. Don't get me wrong I LOVE events, I love putting on new outfits and waiting for what will happen, but

I'm not sorry about a period of respite. The sky sings and
the river keeps flowing toward a waterfall that's about another mile away and that's what happens, that's all that
happens. I've got nothing to do but watch it, and read my
book. I got one of those new editions, where Tom and
Maggie don't have the accident. It's the book and the grass
and the sky. And Wolfe. Just when you start thinking
maybe you'll be alone for the rest of your life.

The calendar on the wall is whispering. I think the
calendar is whispering. Or it's the wind. The calendar if
it's whispering seems to be saying things like daga and
klukkustund, which I swear I can hear but don't understand. You wouldn't expect a calendar in Iceland to speak
English, would you?

I've never felt like this before, like time itself is the only
event and I'm here with it ~~and it doesn't really make me
happy.~~ I don't mean it doesn't make me happy, it makes
the whole idea of happiness feel sort of sweet and small,
like a toy. This is something else, this is a feeling I don't
know the name for and I have the good sense not to try
and come up with a name for it.

I'm sure I'll get better, in another day or so. Mean-
while, it's time for a nap.

PS. I think I see Wolfe, coming up the path.

Love and XXXXX,
Robbie

April 5, 2021

Evening

Darkness comes early to the house in the woods. The house, with a Norway spruce on its southern side and a red oak standing between it and the road, is enfolded in shadow for two or more early-evening hours, depending on the season, while the sky remains bright overhead. For those hours the house's window lights shine under a sky still settling into night, its blue going to lavender, then to twilight, until finally the house and sky inhabit the same darkness.

The sky now is an intricate fretwork of brilliance blazing between the branches and twigs of the spruce and the oak. Isabel's white cotton sweater emits its own faint illumination as she stands on the front porch. Nathan, standing beside her, darkly dressed, is a shadow in the shape of a boy.

Isabel says, "Are you ready for tomorrow?"

"I guess."

"You guys picked out a good place. He'd have liked it."

"How do we know what he would have liked?"

"I knew him pretty well."

She's aware of Nathan's effort to remain silent and contained, to be unflinching, though his breathing goes a bit ragged. She knows not to acknowledge that.

"If you say so."

"He got it in Iceland. He was thousands of miles away. It wouldn't matter if he'd gotten it from you, but he didn't. You had nothing to do with it."

"Violet could have died. Dad could have."

"Violet got better. Your father got better. Your father was hardly sick at all."

"Robbie didn't get better."

"Robbie had a heart condition."

"So does Violet."

"It's more serious if you're older," she says.

Nathan nods, cooperative—he's unfailingly cooperative—but unconvinced. He needs to hear the story over and over. Isabel is willing to tell it to him, over and over. She wishes the repetitions had more effect. She wishes they had any discernible effect at all. Still, she tells him the story again, and again.

"I was the one who let it in," he says.

"You didn't know."

"I did know. I just thought it'd be all right."

"And it *is* all right."

"Not for Robbie."

"Robbie was thousands of miles away. Robbie had a heart condition."

Nathan nods again, resolutely unconvinced.

Does he need, for mysterious reasons of his own, to remain culpable? What can Isabel do, beyond telling him, over and over, that he can release himself?

What child believes his mother when she tells him he's innocent? Isabel's own mother contended that Isabel was guilty of almost everything, which was, unquestionably, a mistake. Isabel envies other mothers, who must be better able to do for their children what their mothers did for them.

And so the story keeps circling back on itself. The reassurances are reiterated. Isabel thinks of rosary beads, the counting of them and the murmured prayers: repeat, repeat, repeat.

Nathan says, "I'm going to go see how Chess and Odin and Garth are doing."

"That'd be good."

"Are you coming inside?"

"In a minute. You go rescue Odin from the adults."

He aims a righteous scowl in her direction. He hates it when she tries to be clever. She's permitted earnestness, affection, and concern, as long as her concerns remain quaint and purposeless, more superstition than science. It matters that she be present, attentive, well-meaning, semideluded, and unable to help him at all.

He turns and opens the door, sending a rectangle of house light onto the floorboards of the porch. Isabel, alone on the porch, watches the sky begin to recede among the branches, go from its sunset incandescence to a lavish pink glow.

Isabel knows the Nathan who exists and she knows the Nathan he's turning into. The child Nathan, the Nathan of last year, was, is, nervous, eager to be liked, and prone to exaggerated mortifications. But this year has brought, for Nathan, an early announcement of childhood's end. The changes are occurring. Nathan and his friends smell different. Their teasings and sparrings have turned from schoolboy incantations to insults, with undercurrents of genuine malice. And, suddenly, much depends on accidents of biology. Harrison has grown three inches. Chad's upper lip has sprouted an outcropping of red-blond hairs.

Nathan has gotten taller, but he's still rounded, still childlike, still more tenor than baritone. Time is threatening to leave him behind. He lives in fear of the day Chad and Harrison make it official: he is someone they used to know. Chad and Harrison will ultimately prove to have been inconsequential (Isabel barely remembers a girl named Marion, who'd been goddess of the eighth grade), but Chad and Harrison, for now, have the power to tell Nathan, *Get over it, dude, you just wanted to hang with us, you didn't know,* an assurance they have yet to offer but might, if Nathan could bear to ask them for it. If Chad and Harrison abandon him, he'll have only his parents and his therapist from whom to withhold everything.

This Nathan, then, still awaiting his own bodily transformations, needs to fully and convincingly inhabit the other Nathan as soon as he can. The new Nathan, already at least halfway conjured, is taciturn, gruff, and only grudgingly affectionate toward others. The new Nathan might be capable of forgiving himself, without the need for Isabel to do it for him.

In the meantime, she does her best to speak to a hybrid of the two. She can see a future in which this revised Nathan is, has long been, the only Nathan, a future in which she pays visits to her gruff, grudgingly affectionate grown son, in which she and Nathan have wordlessly agreed that he was never, not even in childhood, nervous and overeager, never humiliated by other boys.

But this evening, with the ashes soon to be scattered, she knows a Nathan who is no longer his past but not yet his future self—the living specter of her son, quintessence as much as entity, without qualities more specific than anger, self-recrimination, and the fundamental imperishable aliveness Isabel knew of him in utero, the flicker of self that would render him recognizable to her if he died and were reincarnated. She would *know* him, however altered his outward form.

A flatbed truck rattles by, leaves the twin garnets of its tail-lights behind as it jostles down the road that cuts into the black of the woods. Last birds trill in the trees before settling into their nocturnal silence. Isabel watches, listens, strains to hear the owl, though the owl has been silent for weeks. Still, she listens for it. She's lived here for months, but the place refuses to grow familiar. She feels, still, like a traveler who can't quite tell whether her wilderness destination is not what she'd pictured or if she's gone to the wrong wilderness entirely—a place where the nearest neighbor leaves her Christmas decorations out all year, including a life-sized plastic Santa that is illuminated every night; where the opossum that lives under Isabel's house snarls at her when she goes out (what, exactly, is she *doing* here?); where the brown stalks of the ruined vegetable garden, which she still means to replant, rattle in the scoured, watery wind that blows up off the lake.

It might be the wrong place. Or it might be the right place, and her expectations were wrong. It's impossible to tell.

n the living room, Chess sits with Odin on the exhausted old rose-pink armchair with tufts of stuffing protruding along its seams, as if the chair itself were about to abandon the effort required to remain a chair at all. Nathan's mother, here, in this place, buys only that which is already broken and blemished, declaring these things to be treasures, inexplicably abandoned to yard sales and flea markets.

Garth has gone elsewhere. It's only Chess and Odin.

Odin, sitting on Chess's lap, holds Boo, his stuffed rabbit, to Chess's mouth, as if the rabbit were a microphone. Odin goes nowhere without the rabbit. Ever since the day, months ago, that the rabbit was temporarily lost (Garth, late again because his car broke down, an Uber, a doctor's appointment), Odin has been convinced that some quality of the rabbit has remained lost, that this flimsy polyester-furred thing is a zombie of sorts. The rabbit's aliveness remains in possession of the Uber driver who returned it, and Odin is engaged in an endless attempt to summon the rabbit's soul back. Odin insists that others speak through the rabbit to him, that they treat the stuffed animal and the boy as a single being.

Chess is speaking to the rabbit. She speaks with exaggerated urgency, though her words are inaudible. Nathan tries to think of what Chess might feel compelled to say, in a tone of secrecy, to Odin and the rabbit.

She looks up, says, "Hey there, Nathan." Since Nathan let it in, she has tended to speak to him in a low, conspiratorial tone, which resembles the voice she uses when she talks to the rabbit. She speaks to Nathan, speaks *into* him, as she speaks into the eternally astounded face of the stuffed animal.

Nathan nods. He hasn't developed a voice for answering her when she addresses him in the rabbit voice.

She says, "Hey, Odin, look who it is." Odin looks eagerly, if uncertainly, at Nathan—is this guy *still here?* Odin takes the rabbit from Chess's face, holds it out to Nathan.

"Thanks," Nathan says, but when he reaches for the rabbit Odin pulls it tightly to his chest, emits a murmur of displeasure. The rabbit was a greeting, not a gift.

Odin says, "Boo was not like you." Odin hasn't figured out past versus present tense yet but seems generally to prefer the past. Maybe the present is too bright and noisy for him.

"No problem. I don't like Boo much, either."

Odin giggles, as if Nathan has told him a good joke. Odin is only offended when Nathan means not to offend him.

Chess asks Nathan, "Everything all right?"

Nathan wonders, he can't help wondering, why everyone depends on his agreeing that everything's all right.

He says, "Where's Garth?"

"He's around, somewhere."

A hint of strain creeps into Chess's softened, just-you-and-me voice. Something's going on with Garth. But that, it seems, is all right, too.

"I think he went for a walk," she says.

Nathan appreciates the desire, on anyone's part, to go for a walk, to be somewhere other than here, where the living room is a mix of that which makes sense—the signed Patti Smith poster, the rug with the oblongs and triangles, the atmosphere of his mother's soap and perfume—and that which doesn't: the fireplace made of jagged stone shards, the pine floorboards lacquered to a candy-yellow shine, the overhead lamp made of cheap-looking stained glass.

Unlikeliest of all is the box on the stone shelf of the mantelpiece, unremarkable as any other object in the room. It's made of wood, the color of dark chocolate, slightly smaller than a shoebox. There has been, it seems, an effort to render it as ordinary-looking as possible. It sits on the mantel as placidly as the bowl on the coffee table (which contains a spiral notebook, three pinecones, and two decks of cards), as the muddily red-glazed vase from the craft fair in town.

What the box says to the room: Every object, however ordinary, is an artifact of the dead.

Chess says, "You feeling okay about tomorrow?"

"Yeah." There is no other answer to that question.

If Nathan were able to, he'd tell Chess, he'd tell somebody, that he's feeling okay about tomorrow as a concept but is not feeling okay about the place Violet chose, down by the lake. Violet is convinced she's a magical child, able to see that which is invisible to others. Nathan agreed to the place not so much because he truly agreed but because he wanted to conclude, as quickly as possible, the whole excursion, the idea that he and Violet should be in charge of this, when all Nathan wanted was to be taken to the place, wherever it might be, told where to stand and what to do.

At the time, though—when they went out looking, the week before last, on a chill Saturday, rags of snow still white in the shadows—it had seemed right, right enough, what with

Violet's warrior-princess rectitude (*This is his place, right here*) and their mother and father's need for it to be a moment. At the time, it *had* seemed like a moment: the searingly blue sky of late March, the lake blue-black under skittish patches of paper-thin ice, the general impression of a world at pause, preparing to relinquish winter but still holding on, for a while longer, to its clear, cold light, its leafless bushes with their clusters of red berries, nothing buzzing yet, nothing quickening. On a morning like that, during winter's last gasp, Violet's place felt right, right enough. A fitting departure point for the no longer alive. It was only this afternoon that Nathan, walking alone to the spot, caught it in the act of reawakening—the hard knobs on the branches getting ready to burst into green, the lake thawed and glitteringly restive. Here come the blossoms, here come the boats. It's a pretty enough place, but it's neither remote nor remarkable. People will stroll across the grass to get to the lake. It's impossible, now, to think of it as consecrated.

Violet and their father will get here any minute. Could Nathan bring himself to say, *I think we should look for a different place?*

Violet would lose her shit. Violet would need attending to. The scattering of the ashes would become, would be remembered as, a difficult experience for Violet. So much of what happens is revealed to have been a difficult experience for Violet.

Still, Nathan looks out for her, more from duty than devotion. Nathan no longer starts the fights. He does his best to refrain from mocking or humiliating her. He is, after all, the only person who knows about the atmosphere of foreignness in which Violet lives.

There's the foreignness of this house—which has somehow

become their mother's house—and there's the new apartment in Brooklyn, where their father has kept some of the old furniture—the lush, velvety sofa they've had forever, the dented brass bucket that holds magazines, the chest from Japan with its secret drawers—but has also granted entry to the painfully modern wooden chair no one ever sits in, the ancient squares of cardboard with dried weeds taped to them (framed, under glass, as if they were precious), the spindly Italian lamp that doesn't put out any light.

Nathan and Violet go from one strange home to another. It's difficult for both of them, not only for Violet. Has anyone noticed that?

The car's headlights glance dimly across the windows. Its tires crunch on the pine needles.

"Here they are," Chess says.

Here they are. Nathan realizes that his mother has been waiting for them out on the porch, when he'd thought she'd been there for him—he, who is her truest romance, the one who pays attention, who respects her privacy of person (she's not a hug-prone mother; Nathan's okay with that). He took an early train today, on his own. Violet still refuses to be assured that trains are safe.

Nathan thought his mother came out onto the porch with him because she knows, without needing to be told, about the ways in which today and the day before and the day to come evacuate him. Because his mother knows in ways no one else does how impossible it's become for him to reenter the orderly passage of time, how he lives in an ongoing series of minutes that arrive and depart but are not quite fully connected to each other, so that a day is a rapid-fire progression of still photographs, with Nathan as their subject. Here he is in a room with Chess and Odin and a blue rabbit. Here he is, turning to face his father's approaching headlights. He's felt, he's hoped, that his mother knows about it or can guess at it in ways no one else can, not even Doctor Missus Doctor, who gets paid to know about the ways in which Nathan has been emptied, has become photographs of himself. He has no language to convey that. He can only hope someone—if not his mother, someone else—will figure it out. He has no faith in Doctor Missus Doctor, with her *Could you say more* manner, Doctor Missus Doctor, who does not love him, and who dyes her hair a dead black.

His mother loves him. But she hasn't forgiven him, even if she does her best to act as if she has.

D an extinguishes the ignition and turns off the headlights. The house looks more charming, less shabby and desolate, in this purplish semidark. The house could be a life-sized version of a model-railroad house in which human beings can miraculously live, among trees made of styrofoam, behind opaque windows that are simply rectangles of yellow-tinted light, glowing on a train table in somebody's basement.

"Here we are," Dan says.

Violet doesn't answer. She doesn't hurry out of the car, even as Isabel descends the porch steps to meet her. Isabel, smiling determinedly, crosses the stretch of leaf-strewn earth that fronts the house, but Violet remains belted into her seat, as if they had not yet reached the house at all.

She says to Dan, "Do you think Robbie is a ghost?"

That's unexpected.

"I think his spirit is still here," Dan says.

"That's not what I mean."

"I think Robbie will always be with us."

Violet nods, dissatisfied. She's been different since her illness, though it's hard for Dan to be specific, even in his own mind. It's no longer possible to think of Violet only as an innocent little girl, not after she survived her acquaintance with mortality itself; not after she called out to her parents about the strange man who was standing in her room; not after Dan rushed in to find Violet staring in astonishment at an empty corner (the wall on which Jupiter appeared twice, thanks to the careless paperhanger); not after Dan held her and reassured her and—surprise—contracted the illness himself.

On that night, after Violet had cried out, she could see that the figure standing at the foot of her bed was a man and an animal, an animal like a dog but not a dog although it seemed to have velvety white ears like the white Chihuahua's, along with a dog's eager avid attention, but it was also a man, with a man's arms and shoulders. The being, which was hard to see even in the semidark of Violet's room, was strange and yet struck her as familiar. It was not frightening. It seemed to say *grass and stars* but in such a low voice it might have been only the hiss of the radiator that no one would come and fix. Violet, all but involuntarily, started to reach a hand out toward it but before she could extend her hand, before she could tell whether or not the man-dog was going to raise its own hand or paw, her father rushed into her room, the figure dissolved, and there was only her father, holding her, whispering to her that she'd had a bad dream. She let herself be held. Her father was an unmagical creature, doing his best, and she could be helpful to him if she agreed to be a girl who'd had a bad dream.

Violet, recovered, is herself and not quite herself. She isn't morose or angry. She hasn't lost her body of habits and mannerisms. Maybe she's just growing up. Maybe it happens to have coincided with getting sick. She is, whatever the reason, turning into someone who's still effusively polite to others, who still says *hello there* and *how are you* and *goodbye for now* with more brio than the occasion calls for but does so from an inner remoteness no one but her father (and Isabel?) could notice. She's possessed of an innerness. She's acquired a tucked-away quality, as if she's become a Violet who performs as ever but cares less about how her performances are received. A Violet who still wants others to admire her but will survive unharmed if they don't. A Violet who apprehends, for the first time, her own future, in which no one in her present, including her father and mother, will turn out to have mattered all that much.

As Isabel nears the car Violet unbuckles her seat belt, opens the passenger door, and runs to her mother.

Thank you, Violet, for not turning alien on us, not tonight. Thank you for not refusing to get out of the car as it seemed, for a minute, that you might.

Violet will not embrace the habit of refusing to get out of the car for a while yet, and when she does—when she remains obdurately belted in after they've arrived at the dentist and the school play and the Jersey Shore—Dan will be prepared for it. Extracting Violet from cars will have been incorporated by then into their ritual of collaboration and argument.

This evening, though, Violet rushes to her mother, embraces her with such childish glee that it seems to Dan (does Isabel notice it too?) that Violet needed an interval in the car in order to remember how a person like her would act at a time like this.

"Hello, sweetheart," Isabel says. She bends to inhale the scent of Violet's hair. "Did you have a good trip?"

"We saw two dead squirrels and a skunk."

"That's terrible," Isabel says.

Don't make light of it. Every demise matters.

"They don't see the cars coming," Violet says.

Isabel shoots Dan a quick pinprick of a look. *You let her squeeze into that awful dress she's had since she was five? She looks like a miniature crazy person.*

Dan offers the shy smile and the shrug which he hopes by now conveys not only helplessness in the face of ravening forces but a certain Gallic resign. *Who isn't helpless? Isn't it better to acknowledge that? Shouldn't we trade accusation for a more digni-fied, world-weary acknowledgment? We love each other because we can't truly love ourselves, we depend on each other because we can't depend on ourselves. We can't talk our daughters out of ugly dresses that no longer fit, we can't embrace the world the way we once did, we can't stop people from dying.*

"Let's get you inside," Isabel says. "Everybody's here."

"Have you seen Robbie's ghost?"

Isabel was expecting this. She believes she was expecting it. There is, at any rate, a sense of deja vu, Violet referring off-handedly to ghosts and other, less specific spirits and her insis-tence (which she has yet to abandon) that the letters of the alphabet are variously benign and malevolent.

"There's no such thing as ghosts."

"I don't mean a *bad* ghost. I don't mean a *scary* ghost."

"Well, then, yes. His spirit is here. It always will be, wher-ever we are."

"I know," Violet says.

It's surprisingly easy to console her parents. It helps that they think of her as simple. She can play along with that, if it's helpful to them.

She's wearing the yellow dress, which still fits well enough. When she tried it on in the store, she did a pirouette. The gauzy skirt belled out. Robbie applauded. The saleswoman smiled. It was—as Violet will realize, years later—her first true intimation of her own prettiness, of herself as an extraor-dinary being, twirling in the store-light as others smiled and applauded.

The cabin on the mountain in Iceland is empty until the next renters, a French couple, arrive next week. A single square of moonlight lies on the tabletop, its upper right-hand corner interrupted by a can of Five Elephant coffee left there months ago by a German backpacker and a white plate on which someone placed a clump of moss, which has turned yellow and brittle. On one wall, a paper calendar is turned to April 2021. On another hangs a painting of the mountain—depicted as a lopsided green triangle presided over by the white smudge of a cloud—which, hung close to one of the two windows, might have been put there as a demonstration of the disparity between the genuine world and various human attempts to pay homage to it. Two chairs are pulled neatly up to a pine table covered in a floral cloth, a 1960s pattern of daisies, reproduced in vinyl. On the butane stove is an aluminum tea kettle, an enameled saucepan, and a cast-iron skillet. A mouse scurries across the stone floor, pauses with its whiskers twitching, and, sensing nothing of interest, scurries away again. On a wall-mounted coatrack hang a stained suede jacket with fringe running along its sleeves, a brown leather belt, and a faded black T-shirt that says RAMONES over an image of what would once have been an eagle, holding in its talons a leafed branch and what might be a sword or a baseball bat. The bed has been neatly made, with a striped wool blanket folded at its foot. On the wall over the bed hangs a skull, with empty sockets and perfect teeth, beside a shelf that bears variously yellowed copies of old books: *The Magic Mountain, Gone Girl, Snowblind, The Last Duel, The Mill on the Floss.*

C hess finds Garth smoking a cigarette on the back stoop, which is where she expected him to be and what she expected him to be doing. She grew up among men who seemed always to be smoking in the evenings, out behind the house, while the women cleaned up after dinner and swept the floors and put the children to bed.

"Put that out, please," she says.

Garth obediently crushes the cigarette against the concrete, exhales a final plume of smoke. No smoking when Odin is anywhere nearby.

"Sorry," he says.

Seen from behind, sitting on the stoop—his lank blond hair touched here and there by threads of gray, his plaid flannel shirt (vintage, from some shop in the East Village, but still) riding up to show the top of his ass crack—he is revealed, abruptly and unexpectedly, as a member, however far removed, of the man-gaggle that gathered in those long-ago backyards on summer evenings (all of them brothers or cousins or nephews or uncles; it seemed that every man in South Dakota was related, in one way or another, to every other) to complain about their work, their wives, the politicians who were ruining the country. Men who huddled together, laughing gruffly at their own jokes.

Chess says to Garth, "It'd probably be better if you didn't smoke at all while we're here, don't you think?"

"Yeah, it was kind of a minor emergency, won't happen again. Where's Odin?"

"I have no idea where Odin is."

"What?"

"Joke. Bad joke. He's taking a nap. He was getting cranky."

"Who can blame him?" Garth says.

He stands, turns to face Chess. He is not, in fact, a cousin or nephew of those backyard men. Or at least he is only distantly related to them. He stands before Chess in his avid, sculpted beauty, the aging incarnation of the handsome boy who, at Skidmore, persisted in befriending her, a girl just off a bus from South Dakota. Here, decades later, he smiles shyly at her from the narrow, seldom-seen zone of true neglect that lies behind Isabel's house. Out here, on the carpet of pine needles that separates the house from the forest: a dead vegetable garden encircled by sagging chicken wire, two black trash bags full of who knows what, a ladder-back chair with a crooked leg. The chair leans mutely in the unsteady light (the single bulb in the fixture over the back door is burning out), backed by the wall of trees, which, in the flickering light, convey an impression of subtle and furtive movements.

Garth is as timid and hungry as any forest creature. He might have emerged from the woods behind him.

He says again, "Sorry."

"It's all right."

"I mean, about—"

"I know what you mean."

"It's being here. With you and Odin and, you know, and everything. But I shouldn't have said it."

"Maybe it's better that you did."

"I guess I'm thinking about mortality. For, you know, obvious reasons."

"Those creaky old sisters, love and death."

He says, "I know you don't. Feel the same."

"If I did, I think it'd probably be you."

"You *think* it'd *probably* be me?"

"Come on."

"Joke," he says. "Bad joke. What do you think I should do?"

He's been asking variations on that question since they were undergraduates. What do you think I should do about art school? Do you think I should quit my job? What if I broke up with Kate, with Laura, with Rebecca?

"I think you should let it pass," she says.

"I don't know if it will."

"It's not about me."

"Would you mind if I light another cigarette?"

"Please don't," she says. "We agreed. Do you remember that we agreed?"

He glances up at the night sky, to look at something other than Chess. There, in the blackness above, are Castor and Pollux, Betelgeuse, Sirius. Did Garth learn the names of the constellations so as to be more interesting to Chess? Maybe. He's lost track of all he's done to make himself more interesting to Chess.

Looking skyward he says, "I do. I do remember."

Regulus, Arcturus, the cluster of Coma Berenices.

How has he become this poor fuck, hung up on the least likely of romantic fixations after almost twenty years of their shared, jostling comrade-hood—all those private jokes, those confidences and confessions? When, exactly, did the change occur? At what hour, since the day he first chatted her up—the cowgirl who clomped noisily in work boots into their Russian literature class, rough around the eyes and mouth, unapologetically late—and he, young Garth, who was finding that his high school criminal glamour didn't play as well in college, apprehended her peevish, lost-girl defiance and thought, *We should be friends.*

The change did not occur in college. It didn't occur during the year they lived together in the unheated loft on Water Street or while she got him through his coke period and he got her through her depression, or after the summer they were both chasing the same girl.

How is it possible that he's in love with her? How could he have missed his chance, a question further complicated by the fact that there never *was* a chance.

She says, "You're not in love with me."

"Trust me. I've had a lot of experience at not being in love with people. I've been not in love with pretty much everybody, all my life."

"You're not. In love. With me."

"Well, you know, I might be a better authority on how I actually feel. If you don't mind my saying so."

"It's obvious. This is about me as a mother, it's about Odin—"

"I think I've been in love with you for a long time. I think I just . . . didn't see it. I've been pretty distracted. Since I was about fifteen years old."

"Fucking every woman in New York City. Since you were about fifteen years old."

"Not *all* of them. A pretty small percentage, really."

Chess says, "I've been offered a job at Berkeley."

"Oh."

"It's a good offer. More money, fewer classes."

"When were you going to tell me?"

"I'm telling you now. I just heard about it a few days ago."

"What are you going to tell Berkeley?"

"I haven't decided yet."

"What about me?"

That's always the question, isn't it? No matter how abject and adoring he may be, underneath there's always the question *What about me?*

She says, "If I take the job, you could move to California with us."

For an interlude it's them in the night together, with its faint rustlings and its buzz of insects. The faltering light over the back door is haloed by gnats.

"If I was to move to California—" he says.

"I didn't mean it. You shouldn't move to California."

"You said it, though."

"Rewind. Erase."

"You're right, I shouldn't, that'd be weird. But when would I see Odin?"

"There are flights to California. Every day."

Chess is not sure why she needs to be cruel to him. She does, however, need to be, at the moment.

"Got it," he says. "I'm going to go for a drive."

"Do you think that's a good idea?"

"I'm not going to drive into a tree or anything. I just need to be . . . not here, for a while."

"Garth?"

"Yeah?"

"Don't do this to me."

"This is something I'm doing to *you*?"

Here, then, is the answer. A degree of cruelty is necessary because Garth, like most men, can only deposit his needs at her feet, can only declare his love—that romantic hallucination, which would begin to fade as soon as she said yes—can only say, *Here is my desire, here is my loneliness, what are you going to do about it?*

"Never mind," she says. "Go for a drive."

"Yep. See you later."

After he's gone, Chess remains standing in the doorway. She's not ready to go back inside, not yet. She knows that in Garth's eyes, and in the eyes of others, she has become Garth's de facto wife; that by allowing Garth to know Odin, to have a voice and a vote, she's agreed to a union that looks like marriage—enough like marriage—to be taken up, encouraged, sentimentalized, because the world wants women to marry men, the world prefers it that way, still does, always has. It's one of the favorite stories. *She used to be with women until that guy came along,* until she confessed that men are, after all, compelling and necessary, that they are neither self-obsessed nor so enamored of their own feelings that they, along with the world, mistake those feelings for love.

It would be easier if she were more innocent. It would be easier if she felt surer about the lines that separate pity from desire, and desire from rage. She does not love men. She does not love Garth. And yet something keeps shifting inside her, a queasiness that's not love but is not nothing and maybe, in its way, is not exactly, not entirely, not love.

There is the question of dinner. Isabel has chickens and potatoes and a salad. She bought the chickens from a farmer two towns away, the lettuces—escarole and arugula and frisée—from the farm market. She got lost in the particulars, in questions of integrity and freshness, but now that it's all here, now that the chickens, three of them, rest in the big roasting pan, now that the potatoes have been scrubbed and the lettuce is in the refrigerator, it all strikes her as pointless effort, and she strikes herself as a ridiculous person, someone who thinks that farm-raised chickens and local lettuces will matter, when no one would notice, no one would care, if she'd just picked it all up at the Stop & Shop.

She's preheated the oven. It's time to put the chickens in, but she stands staring at them in the pan on the stovetop, their pimpled skins, their wings tucked discreetly under their breasts. Their wings are longer and scalier than those of supermarket chickens, which, as everybody knows, are mutated in ways you'd rather not think about, even the "organic" ones. These chickens, with their longer wings and smaller breasts, with the stub of a pinfeather Isabel has had to pluck from one of their legs, were more apparently once alive. They were more apparently swept up in a chaos of noise and feathers, beheaded, and plucked. They attest, in their blue-white silence, to slaughter, and the quietude after. It seems overly dramatic to think of them as alien babies. They are, however, like alien babies, even if it *is* overly dramatic.

Isabel herself is insufficiently dramatic—taciturn, more than a little coldhearted, someone who shops at the farm market in hope of becoming more convincingly the kind of person who shops at the farm market, the kind of person who's at home among all the women and men who've brought their own bags (she herself never remembers), who are jovial and self-satisfied, unconcerned about themselves as members of the newly rural rich, hybrids of farmer and financier, who speak as knowledgably about the first of the fiddlehead ferns as they do about net worth and capital gains.

The box is on the mantel in the living room. Isabel is in the kitchen. It's time for her to start making dinner.

She takes Robbie's phone out of her pocket, chooses another of his photographs. Isabel is Wolfe, now. She feels no guilt about it, she who feels guilty about almost everything else. Robbie would want, as does Isabel, for Wolfe to live on.

She doesn't need to account, on Instagram, for Robbie and Wolfe's meeting, though she's told herself they met at a party to which Robbie was dragged unwillingly by friends who promised him he could leave again after he'd had one drink and talked to one person. Robbie dutifully poured a splash of cheap vodka into a red plastic cup and started speaking to Wolfe simply because Wolfe was the person standing closest to the makeshift bar. If Robbie hadn't been on an assignment he'd never have had the nerve to speak to Wolfe, who was too genially confident, too tall.

Robbie made some remark about the ubiquity of those red plastic cups at parties, did Wolfe think they had them in Argentina and China, too?

Wolfe had been to Argentina and you know they really do have these red plastic glasses there . . .

He and Wolfe started talking. They never stopped.

Isabel wants that explanation. It doesn't matter to Instagram. Instagram doesn't require narratives. The gaps between images can go unexplained. The implication suffices: just like that, Wolfe found the man he'd been waiting for. Just like that, Robbie found him, too.

Image: An Icelandic landscape, a field of black stone punctuated by outcroppings of phosphorescent green moss and brilliantly blue thermal pools. It's the least earthly possible place on the surface of the planet. It could be the surface of another planet altogether, one that might disappoint interstellar travelers in their hopes for fecundity—for jungles teeming with unknown creatures, winged or hooved or both—but that offers instead a stark and severe grandeur that equals, in its way, any offering of fern or frond. Didn't Robbie write, in that long-ago letter, about Iceland as a kind of heaven, even if it would have disconcerted poor old Aunt Zara, who'd have wanted to know if there'd been some mistake, if she who'd lived a pious and righteous life had been sent to the wrong afterlife.

Caption: Robbie and I are in heaven together. Here, in the middle of everywhere.

Isabel still marvels occasionally over the fact that none of Wolfe's followers seem to notice, or care, that Wolfe (and now Robbie, alongside him) has been in Iceland for over a year. It is, she supposes, a kind of eternity for Robbie and Wolfe. An escape from the boundaries of time.

No one suspects that Nathan has slipped away and gone to the lake. Nobody noticed. He's less astonished than he used to be by the fact that people seem to believe him when he assures them that he's all right. He's mostly stopped blaming them for it. Why wouldn't they want one less person to worry over?

He lies on his back on the brittle grass, watching the sky, its swarming of stars.

This place is less prosaic at night. Maybe it's not the wrong spot, after all.

He props himself on his elbows, looks down the small rise to the lake. Here is this place, alone with itself. Here are its trees with their faint tarry smell. Here is its expanse of calm water. Here is its sky and its silence.

He can't be forgiven. He knows that.

He stands, walks to the edge of the lake. The stars are so bright that a few, the most brilliant, shimmer skittishly on the black surface of the water.

What if he waded in? What if he swam to the nearest of the stars?

He bends over, scoops water into his hands. It's even colder than he'd expected it to be. He dislikes the fact that he fears, more than anything, the coldness of the water. He takes a half step forward, plunges his hands back into the water. It laps at the toes of his Nikes. He feels sure he can get past his fear of the cold if he gives himself more time. An owl murmurs from somewhere across the lake, so softly you could mistake it for the sound of the lake itself—the lake's wistful sigh. He steps into the water, up to his calves. The lake's bottom is silty; it sucks at the soles of his shoes. The water is so dark it's as if his lower legs have disappeared. He can wade into his fear of the cold. He feels sure that he can. He takes another step forward. A star flickers on the water's surface. The owl hoots again, from the lake's far shore.

sabel has written Wolfe's caption, posted image and caption, when Dan comes into the kitchen. She slips the phone back into her pocket.

Dan says, "You okay?"

"Mm-hm."

She doesn't turn to him. A truth about your estranged husband: you no longer have to consider his feelings. Even if your parting was courteous, more admission of shared defeat—love has reached its conclusion—than battle. Even if you're still friends, or whatever term you choose for what you've become to each other.

"Are you going to put the chickens in?" he asks.

"I am."

She holds her elbows close to her sides. She can tell Dan has stepped closer to her by the minor magnification of his smell, the brisk, salty tang of his sweat mingled with what she can only think of as *Dan,* which resembles the smells of metal and cedar shavings but is not quite either of the two. Now that they see each other less, she's more aware of his smell.

He says, "Why don't I take care of dinner?"

"Are you sure?"

"I'm sure."

She turns to him. She is briefly unsettled by his ruddy, weathered good looks, even though she saw him less than twenty minutes ago. It's as if the Dan she's always known has undergone some last-minute transformation, grown older and more attractive, his own personal volume knob turned ever so slightly up. His hair is electrically blond only at the outermost tips. His mouth is bracketed by two deeply etched lines that not only emphasize the softness of his lips but lend them an element of kissable authority they lacked in his younger, prettier face. He is handling, with unanticipated good humor, the fact that his comeback was not only minor, but has come and gone. He hasn't needed, as it turns out, the bucking up Isabel dreaded being asked to provide. She asks herself sometimes how much their parting had to do with her own reluctance to see Dan through the evaporation of his hopes, her trepidations about the prospect of finding him still in bed in midafternoon, waiting for her to offer whatever she could offer about the gift of being alive, of loving and being loved—all the supposed verities about which she is unsure, herself.

That Dan, however, failed to arrive.

This Dan is pleased, pleased enough, with his short-lived semi-success, considers it a job well done, and is, or so it seems, roughly as pleased to be teaching at the New School. This Dan is unbothered by the fact that Isabel still earns most of the money. This Dan is pleased, as well (or seems to be), by his younger brother's equally unanticipated success: Garth's show at the gallery on Orchard Street, the purchase of a piece by the Whitney. The Whitney, for reasons best known to itself, wanted a sculpture called *Hamlet,* covered in pigskin coated with tar, its recesses studded with pebbles of broken glass, fake diamonds, and the teeth Garth ordered online—weird that anyone can order something like that.

Mysteriously, Garth appears to have aged since he became successful. Words like "sallow" and "drawn" had never come to mind, before. Dan, mildly accomplished but still, essentially, failed, is as solid and sure-looking as if he'd been carved from pink granite.

She wonders how many women think more kindly and, all right, more lustfully toward their husbands after they've left them. Maybe someone's done a study. Maybe you could Google it.

"Sit over there," he says, indicating the oak stool she bought at the shabby antiques store that went out of business a week after she bought it, another of those places that somehow survived the worst and then collapsed during the aftermath.

She sits on the stool. He takes a bottle of cabernet from the countertop, knows somehow in which drawer the corkscrew is kept.

He says, "This kitchen is nice."

The kitchen is the house's only inarguable virtue. Isabel, not quite fully lucid when she rented the house, knew only that she needed to live for a while in the country, and that she needed a place with bedrooms for the children. All the others she saw were imitations of country houses: wainscoting painted in minty pastels, newly installed oak floors, recently added three-car garages.

When Isabel said to the real estate agent, "I think we need to look at places that aren't so haunted by their own unhauntedness, if you know what I mean," the agent responded with a smile of baffled irritation. When Isabel added, "Something more old-fashioned, something a little less fixed up," the quality of the agent's smile shifted. Here, as she'd tell her husband over cocktails that night, was someone who might rent the place on Skinner Road.

After Isabel moved into the place on Skinner Road, it took her only a short while to realize that *a little less fixed up* can be discouraging in its own right, when it means that the previous denizens have shellacked the pine floors, left an ineradicable smell of dog in the basement, and glued acoustic tiles onto the ceilings of the upstairs bedrooms. If the other houses were sentimental reinventions of country life, their histories scrubbed away, the place on Skinner Road stubbornly retains its own history of desolation and long, drunken nights, of whatever sequence of unfortunate choices and bad luck have landed others here. When Isabel first agreed to the house, she underestimated its lingering air of dank disappointment, as well as her own inability to do much of anything about it. She only knows that after she got the call about Robbie she needed to go away, to live for a while in solitude, in a place close enough to the children (less than an hour's drive, without traffic) but where she would not be encouraged to get out more, to go for walks or meet a friend for lunch. Most people, even (or especially) those who care most about you, will permit you a month or two of mourning before they start growing impatient, on your behalf, and on theirs.

And, as Isabel is reminded tonight, she was seduced by the house's kitchen, where the ancient Art Deco–ish refrigerator and stove are still functional, where the old beamed ceiling remains, as does the red linoleum floor that's been here fifty years or more. Most of the house's previous occupants probably didn't care much about cooking. It's easy to picture the kitchen sink piled with dirty dishes on which take-out meals were hastily consumed, the counters piled with empty pizza boxes, which, once they've been removed, have left the kitchen un-troubled, pristine in its way, needing only a less-than-100-watt lightbulb screwed into its fluted overhead fixture. Isabel was able to manage that.

Dan opens the wine, pours some into a juice glass, and hands it to her. The cabernet is so dark as to be nearly black. She takes a sip and feels, fleetingly, that she's never tasted anything quite so delicious.

Dan says, "Have the chickens been salted, or anything?"

"Not really. I mean, I was about to."

"No worries. I'm on it."

He takes the cylinder of salt from the counter, pours some into the palm of his hand, and rubs it onto the chickens. They'd be as thoroughly salted if he'd shaken the salt directly from its container, but Dan prefers to handle food, to address it physi-cally, massage it into the most delicious possible manifestation of itself.

He says, "I'm still amazed how quiet and dark it is here, at night."

"There was an owl for a while, down by the lake. You could hear her hooting if you really listened for it, but she seems to have moved on. Unless something *got* her. Do you think there are animals that eat owls?"

"Hard to say."

Dan opens the refrigerator, finds a couple of lemons and a bunch of parsley that's only slightly wilted. Isabel doesn't mind about Dan seeing her capacity for neglect. She does her best to conceal it from everybody else but, as far as Dan is concerned, she finds some peculiar solace in letting him see how bad it really is.

He says, "It's lonely here, isn't it?"

She overcomes a hiccup of irritation. *You're worried about my loneliness* now*?*

She says, "Lydia thinks I came here so there'd be a place for Robbie."

He chops the parsley, stuffs it into the chickens' cavities along with the lemons. "It makes sense," he says. "Do you think it makes sense?"

"Kind of. And kind of not. I also came here to get out of Brooklyn. I'm not just here on some kind of mission for Robbie."

"I know."

"But, yes. I may have, partly, wanted a place for him. He never really had much of a place."

"Do you still feel bad about that?"

"Yeah, of course I do," she says. "Don't you?"

A silence passes. Dan is still entitled to much from her, but he's relinquished his rights to consolation. Helping Dan feel better about his acts and omissions is no longer part of her job.

Dan says, "Violet asked me if Robbie's ghost is here."

"She asked me, too. What did *you* tell her?"

"That his spirit is everywhere."

"I said pretty much the same thing. She didn't buy it, did she?"

"No," he says.

"But I think. I think that might be okay. Okay being a relative concept. But, you know. Vi insisting that he's not just totally *gone*."

The Icelandic police were kind and gentle over the phone. They assured Isabel and Dan that Robbie looked peaceful when they found him, but they could not, or would not (police are police), answer Isabel's more detailed questions. Was he covered with a blanket? Did he have a book in his hands? Of all the impossibilities, one of the least tenable is the idea of Robbie alone in that cabin. If she'd been there with him . . .

She can't have been there with him. She can only hope that it was like falling asleep. She can't purge herself of her own fears about how untrue that might be, though she can set them aside. Sometimes, she can set them aside.

She says, "Nathan is having second thoughts about the place we picked out, for tomorrow."

"He didn't tell me that."

"He didn't exactly tell me, either. But it's pretty obvious."

"Do you think we should look for another place, in the morning?"

"I think that'd make it worse. I think Nathan will be all right. And do *you* want to have that conversation with Violet?"

Dan opens the oven. It exhales a blast of heat. Isabel takes a sip of the wine. It's already less astonishing, more like regular wine.

She says, "You let her stuff herself into that godawful dress."

"No, I lost the argument when she reminded me that it's the last thing Robbie bought her."

Isabel sips her wine, rolls it around in her mouth. "Right."

"It's hard to know what to do," Dan says.

"Tell me about it."

Dan lifts the pan from the stovetop, slides it into the oven. "Off you go, girls."

Isabel says, "They're not girls."

"Come again."

"They're chickens. Dead chickens. They're not girls."

Dan pours himself a glass of wine. "Why are you being like this?" he says.

"Sorry. I'm . . . unnerved."

"Me too. Does it seem like I'm doing fine?"

"Do you think we should have invited Oliver?"

"Uh, the Oliver who broke up with Robbie in a text? Probably not."

"What about Adam?"

"In the card he sent he didn't ask about whether there'd be a memorial."

"I know. I just hate it that . . ."

"You hate it that there's no boyfriend or anyone like that, here."

"You know how much I like it when you finish my sentences for me."

"Sorry," he says. "*I* hate it that Robbie wasn't in love when he—"

"Died. When he died. That's the word for what happened to him."

"You know how much I like it when you correct my vocabulary. But, yeah."

"At least my father's not around anymore. Not that I don't miss him."

"I know you miss him."

"But I don't miss the fight we'd have had about not burying Robbie next to Dad and Mom."

"Why would anybody want to have *that* fight?"

"No one would," she says. "Okay. I've got a slightly difficult question."

"Shoot."

"Do you think Robbie was ever in love? With any of those guys?"

"Adam," he says. "I think he may have been in love with Adam."

"Hard to argue with a pretty boy who played the cello."

"Remember the night he came to dinner and played the Bach cello suite for us?"

"It's not like I'd forget about that."

"But then Adam met the violinist. And that was that."

"He did send that card," she says.

"Two lines about sympathy, and what a great guy Robbie was. No further questions."

"Right. But didn't Adam seem like . . . more of a *person,* like somebody who'd do more than send a card?"

"Musicians," Dan says. "Most of us aren't such great bets. Present company excepted."

"I've got another difficult question."

"I'm all ears."

"I've never brought this up before."

"Now is probably the time, then."

"Have you ever noticed that all Robbie's boyfriends looked like you?"

"What?"

"How could you not have noticed?"

"Maybe because it isn't true."

"Come on. Blond. Musicians."

"Oliver wasn't a musician."

"DJ. Minor difference."

"What are you getting at?"

"I'm not quite sure."

"Give it a try."

"Well. It's too simple and obvious to say Robbie was in love with you."

"Robbie and I *were* in love with each other. But I hope you don't think we ever—"

"No. I don't think that. Of course I don't. Don't take this the wrong way, but I'm not sure if Robbie was exactly *in love* with you."

"Thanks."

"I don't mean it to be insulting. Robbie loved you. It isn't that."

"What is it?" he says.

"Remember when you took him on that cross-country drive?"

"To see the world's second-largest ball of twine."

"He told me he'd never been so happy."

"Which he also said when each of the kids were born. And, I think, when he got that embroidered velvet Dries Van Noten jacket for seventy percent off."

"Please don't joke about this."

"I'm not. I'm trying to put this into a little bit of perspective, is all."

"You know how much I like it when you put things into perspective."

"I just think . . ." he says.

"Let's let this one go, okay?"

"Or not."

She says, "I think Robbie was looking for someone who'd thrill him the way you did on that drive. Which I *do* think may have been the happiest time of his life. Well, maybe tied with the velvet jacket. I mean, *seventy percent* off?"

"Do you honestly think Robbie spent twenty years chasing

after something that happened for a few days when he was seventeen?"

"I don't think he *knew* that."

"Not exactly an answer."

"I'm not sure if you know how gorgeous you were, then."

"As opposed to how I am now."

"If you're determined to be insulted."

"All right," he says. "I'm not insulted. But I would like to think maybe I'm not some kind of burnt-out hulk."

"Robbie was seventeen. Nobody knew he was gay. Well, I knew, but we never talked about it, not then. Nobody was in love with him yet."

"What are you trying to say?"

"I think he'd have gotten over it. That thing about blond music boys. If he'd had more time."

Isabel finishes her wine. She returns to a day more than twenty years ago.

Robbie is seventeen. Dan is twenty. They're back from seeing the world's second-largest ball of twine. They're both coated in road grime, both flushed with excitement, though Dan plays it semi-cool while Robbie is ecstatic, rife with stories. The motel bed with Magic Fingers, which, when you inserted a coin, made the bed jiggle for ten minutes. The two hitchhiking sisters on their way home from a Civil War reenactment where they'd been nurses tending to the wounded. The diner with the sign that said, SAVE US JESUS.

Isabel expected all that. Robbie's glee, his teenage tales of the road.

But there's something else ... Isabel barely notices it at first ...

Robbie has taken on a more fluent presence. He's shed some

measure of his own hesitancy. He occupies the air differently. It's a change so minute that only Isabel would notice it at all. He stands more squarely. His voice is neither louder nor deeper, but there's a new underlayer of conviction, as if he no longer doubts that others are listening to him as he tells of Magic Fingers and Civil War nurses.

Could having spent a couple of days on the road with Dan have made a difference in Robbie? It seems that it has.

The travelers, returned, stand with Isabel on the front lawn of Isabel and Robbie's parents' house. Dan's car is parked in the driveway, the wreck of it an affront to the house's prim clapboard rectitude, its dormers and hydrangea bushes. Robbie says, "Next time we'll go see the *largest* ball of twine."

"Or we could go see the smallest one," Dan says.

They have themselves a laugh, together. Isabel can picture them driving along a stretch of highway with the windows open and the music blasting, a parade float cut off from the rest of the parade, come to wish the country a snatch of passing rock and roll, to wish freedom and recklessness upon the fields of Pennsylvania, the foothills of Ohio.

They must have irritated the locals as they caromed along. They must have been thrilled by themselves, by the lives that permitted them this. They must have been lost in the spirited self-regard available only to boys while they're still young— the innocent grandeur of self that can't last, or shouldn't last, beyond early youth.

There is, or so it seems, a world of boys, into which girls are not invited. Even if the boys in question love girls. Even if they prefer them to other boys.

Twenty-year-old Dan drapes an arm over Isabel's shoulders.

He says softly to her, "The dude and I had some fun together," as Robbie sings, *And I shall drive my chariot down your streets and cry.*

Standing with Dan's arm around her and Robbie singing his song, Isabel thinks, for the first time since she and Dan met, that this tale-telling exaltation, the boys' fit of home-again hilarity, is something she might try to enter, against all the odds. She takes Dan's hand in hers, presses his index finger to her lips, as Dan joins Robbie in singing, *Hey it's me I'm dynamite and I don't know why.*

Here, in the kitchen, Dan says, "We all wish he'd had more time."

"We all wish that, yes."

"We're boats borne into the past. Fitzgerald."

"I know it's Fitzgerald. The line is 'borne back ceaselessly into the past.' Something like that."

"Something like that."

He opens the oven door, takes a look at the chickens.

"Thank you," she says. "For cooking the chickens."

"It's no big deal."

"I have a feeling I might have stood there, staring at them, until somebody came in and took over."

"And I'm the guy."

"You're the guy."

Dan waits. He waits for Isabel to ask about him. How is he doing? Doesn't she know—how could she fail to know—that Robbie was the love of his life? Could she possibly think that Robbie mattered less to Dan because Dan isn't gay? Would she be angrier but more empathic if Dan and Robbie had been covert lovers?

Is it only going to be *Thanks for making dinner* and *How do you think the kids are doing* and *Was Robbie ever in love?*

It is. For now. For tonight, and maybe forever. Dan is egocentric, and emotionally venal. He knows that. He does know that. He knows how little claim he has. He knows he can't ask Isabel to take him on as if he were a third child. Which doesn't prevent him from wanting her to do exactly that.

He says, "Would you like more wine?"

"I would."

He pours more wine for her. She looks up at him. He looks questioningly back at her. He knows that she knows how brave he's being, for her sake and for the sake of the kids. He knows how grateful she is, as she knows he knows about the sacrifices, the generosities, the fatigued forgiveness they can offer to each other.

They might find a way. They might be able to return. They could revive it, resurrect it. They never, after all, fell entirely *out* of love, they merely slipped away from love, lost track of it. They didn't hire lawyers, didn't fight over money or custody. And so, for a tick of the clock, it seems they could resuscitate it, with new agreements and renewed vows. They could move back in. They could pay closer attention and perform daily mercies and live, merely live, through whatever time it would take . . .

Isabel is the first to look away. She says, "Thank you."

"For what?"

"Being here, I guess."

"Did you think I *wouldn't* be here?"

"No. I didn't think that."

Another silence descends. An aperture has closed. There's

no return for them, nothing left to rekindle. Isabel knows it. They can go on being cordial and affectionate. They can worry together about the children. They can even desire happiness, each for the other, but they are no longer lovers, they are no longer married, which, by way of a transition, is all the more final for having escaped their attention, for having occurred in increments, like a leak that goes undetected until the day it becomes apparent that the whole structure has been saturated, so full of moisture and mildew that it can no longer be repaired.

When Violet announces that she's going upstairs with her suitcase, no one asks her if she'll be all right up there on her own, which is a relief. She is too often accompanied.

Violet needs to be by herself, at present. She's had the good sense not to mention the shadow she saw, a few minutes earlier, slipping by the living room window. It might have been Robbie or it might have been another shade, wandering past. The world is full of shadows, some of them purposeful, some confused or lost, some so formless as to be not much more than fleeting disturbances on a pane of window glass. Since Violet has learned to see them, after that first visitation when she was sick and the gentle dog-man came to her, she can barely remember a time when shades and improbable beings were as invisible to her as they are to others.

Her upstairs bedroom, with its canted ceiling and dormer window, is meant to be comfortable, and comforting. An effort has been made. There's the white bed with its flourish of leaves carved into the headboard. There's the shepherdess with a lamp coming out of her head, the curtains dotted with thumbnail-sized roses. Although Violet hasn't mentioned it, she feels, when she's here, that she uses the bedroom temporarily, until the arrival of the girl for whom it's intended. Violet prefers it this way. Everything about this house, all its rooms and their contents, is a memory. It's a place Violet used to be.

She sets her suitcase, unopened, on the bed.

The curtains are closed. Violet's mother has a habit of clos-ing up for the night: curtains drawn, doors locked, all the cush-ions brought in from the chairs on the front porch, because you never know if it might rain.

Violet goes to the window, opens the curtains. The curtain rings rattle. She looks out into the woods behind the house. The woods are alive with the spirits of animals and the dreams of trees, most active at night, when the dreams and the spirits are most fully awake, when they drift across the forest floor, murmuring in wordless languages they themselves don't fully understand, searching, confused, as the planets shine down from among the leaves and the houses glow so faintly as to be invisible to anyone who does not live in them.

Violet is sorry, sometimes, that no one else can see any of it, that they live in a more obvious and less interesting world. Her father didn't notice, on the drive here, that one of the squirrels in the road still shone faintly with the last strain of its already-extinguished life. When Violet and her father arrived, her mother didn't notice that her father remained silent, because he has a secret. There's no telling what the secret might be— Violet's vision doesn't penetrate like that—but she could see the secret itself in his slightly reddened face, she could hear it in what he didn't say.

Still. No one else needs to see or hear what Violet sees and hears. It may be better for her, for everyone, if they don't.

She stands at the window with her palms spread on the sill, waiting.

sabel posts again on Instagram. It's one of her favorites, from Robbie's file.

Image: The photo was taken inside the cabin, looking out through a window. The window is bracketed by murky brown curtains. On the sill are an empty cut-crystal vase, a few coins, and a dark gray stone the size of a baby's shoe. Outside, though: a field of grass that slopes downward to what would be a valley but appears, in the picture, to be a dropping off into a void filled only with the pale, misty blue of a sky that turns, in its upper reaches, to an almost violent blue. The sky offers a single white cloud, compact and well-defined, no incident of furl or softening at its edges, a companion of sorts to the stone on the windowsill.

Isabel can pass easily through the Instagram portal. She can picture herself there with Robbie, in a photograph taken a year ago. She can be there with him in the cabin, though she can't see much. The cabin is difficult to piece together, from the photographs. There are only shots of a table's edge, of a skull nailed to a wall beside a bookshelf, and a bed barely big enough for two, above which hangs the shelf, lined with books the titles of which are not legible in the photograph. She knows, however, that when Robbie took this picture he'd have been aware, as is she, of the corollary between the rock and the cloud.

> Caption: We wouldn't be all that surprised if there were a knock on the door and it turned out to be an entity cloaked in moss, with a kindly and inquisitive face under a hat made of ferns, who was only stopping by to see us, to know that we're here, to welcome us and to wish us prosperity and long life.

She hesitates. It isn't Wolfe's voice. Wolfe is poetic in his heart but is not given to lyrical flights. He's too abashed, too prone to venerations to try to put them into words. Wolfe knows that words fail. He knows that his life and Robbie's life are better contained in gestures, in a hand placed gently on a face, in an unexpected kiss or a whispered endearment, ephemeral, as impossible to speak of as they are to photograph.

She's the one who strives to explain. She's the one who refuses to accept the idea that there's anything one person can't say to another.

She thinks of rewriting the caption, decides against it, sends it out.

Garth hadn't expected Isabel's "house in the country" to be moldy and dank, any more than he'd expected the country itself to be an endless swath of pine forest, gathered around a lake but devoid of meadow or mountain, claustrophobic (it offers no horizons, only infinities of trees), fretted with narrow roads that lead to other narrow roads, punctuated by human settlements that range from trailers on cinder blocks to faux farmhouses to a few mini-palaces with turrets and bay windows. As Garth drives from road to road, as his headlights illuminate the variously homemade plaques that announce the roads' names (Whispering Glen, Lakeview, Latches Lane), he struggles to picture himself when he returns to Isabel's house, if he can ever find it again. What will he find to say to Chess that isn't merely more cringing apology and further protestations of hopeless love? He wants to tell her, in a way that'll make sense, that he couldn't bear living on the outside for the past year, that he can't stand being quite this unnecessary, can't bear the fact that Chess and Odin are all right without him. But he knows how that will land. He knows it's only manspeak to Chess. But he feels himself diminishing. There's been less and less of him since Chess locked herself in with Odin, and it seems to Garth that if he doesn't say something that registers, if he doesn't do something meaningful, he'll live on as a missing person, even if he's missing only to himself. He'll be more uncle than father, the guy who takes you to the park and buys you that toy your mother forbids. Someone like Robbie. Garth will be a peripheral figure in life as Robbie is in death.

Garth can't move to California only because Chess is moving there. It'd be awkward under any circumstances, and it's impossible now that his career is taking off. This is not the time for an artist to leave New York. It's not a time when an artist can fail to show up at dinners and parties, to talk to curators and collectors, to work his charms. Garth has been at it too long to think that the work is perceived independently of the artist who made it. It matters that the artist—Garth is good at this—can talk about genesis and process, about vision, while sipping from a champagne flute, wearing jeans and a tuxedo jacket, smelling faintly of paint and a hint of cologne. Seduction figures in. It'd be naïve to think otherwise.

What will he do, though, if Chess and Odin move away?

This reaction, this low howl of loss, this yearning to be a father, is the last thing Garth expected.

He turns onto another road, into still more forest, more windows putting out their squares of light among the trunks of trees. He keeps driving, turns from one identical road onto another, and then another.

Once Nathan has gone into the water, it's so dark and cold he can't tell the cold from the dark. He needs only to swim on. He's not sure if he's swimming away from something or more deeply into something, but he has to keep moving through the dark cold, if only because he couldn't continue standing on the bank of the lake, where Robbie's ashes will be scattered tomorrow morning, and he couldn't go back to the house. He couldn't return to the warmth and the light. He couldn't *talk* to anyone, couldn't withstand their demonstrations of love and sympathy. He doesn't want to hate them any more than he does already. He swims underwater through the dark cold into more dark cold, farther and farther, though there is no sense of progression, only his strokes and kicks, the downward pull of his clothes and his shoes into the slightly deeper darkness below. His fingers seem to have been welded together. His hands are paddles, cupping the water. He glances up at the skin of lesser dark overhead, the water's unbright surface, checking to see if the star's reflection might be skimming along with him but, seeing no star, he swims on into more of it, into something that's a destination but not a place, not exactly a place: an absence he's disappearing into, where he'll swim out of himself and be no one, where he'll be gone, just gone, only gone.

sabel finds Chess sitting in the damaged chair behind the house. Isabel had hoped no one would venture out there. She'd meant to get it cleaned up.

She says, "That chair isn't really safe to sit in."

"I've survived it so far. I should go check on Odin."

"He's fine, he's still asleep. Dan is watching him."

"Garth went for a drive."

"Is he——"

Chess shifts her weight in the chair, which emits a small, creaturely squeal.

"We're working it out," she says.

There is, after all, nothing for Chess and Garth to do but *work it out*. Still, Chess can't help thinking about how, or if, she went wrong.

You ask your college friend for a teaspoonful of his essence, thinking, *We can live compassionately in a future we devise for ourselves.* It was not an obvious mistake. Garth could retain his freedom and fecklessness. He'd be a man for Odin to know, the resident answer to the paternity question, as Odin grew up. Garth would have his two days a week, he'd be mildly fatherly according to his limitations, and would otherwise mind his own business.

Chess didn't expect him—heedless and self-involved, the art guy with the Ducati—to think he was falling in love. She didn't imagine he'd imagine himself as her husband.

"It's never easy," Isabel says.

"Here's the joke, though. I thought it would be. Not *easy*, but it did seem . . . like it'd be the baby and me, with my friend Garth there to help out."

"Well, all right, I guess I thought, when I married Dan, that we'd be . . . that it would be at least relatively kind of . . . semi-easy."

"Women always know better, though. Don't you think?"

"I think you think it'll be different, for you. You think you're not like other women."

Chess emits a raucous hoot of a laugh. "I've always felt fairly confident that I'm not all that much like other women."

Isabel laughs in return, though her laugh is softer and more tentative. She says, "Do you think we all think we're not all that much like other women?"

"I guess that's the story, isn't it? We all think we're not like other women."

Isabel says, "And yet, here we are."

"And yet, I feel like I'm partly responsible. For this. Thing of Garth's."

"Do you?"

"I feel like I gave him *room* for it. Like, I never encouraged him, but maybe I didn't discourage him enough."

"We should be better friends. Don't you think?"

"Sure," Chess says. "Except for the fact that we don't really like each other all that much."

"I don't see why that should stop us from being friends. How many friends really like each other?"

"It does get lonely," Chess says.

"And you get tired."

"You do."

"We should go back in."

"I hope I can get out of this chair."

"I didn't expect anyone to *sit* in it."

"What's it doing out here in the first place?"

"One of its legs is broken."

"I see that."

"I keep thinking I'm going to get it fixed."

"You're not going to get it fixed."

"But I can't seem to get rid of it, either. We should go back inside. It's almost time for dinner."

"We should."

They hesitate. It seems that they share a secret but the secret can't be spoken. The secret is this, the two of them, silent together, weary and vigilant, unaccompanied in the world although they are not alone in it; waiting, both of them, for something to collapse: the chair, the house, the economy; alert to the possibility of distant sounds: an approaching car, a whimpering child; two people who can't stop paying attention, ever; who are compelled to worry about the future because the future threatens to unmake their children. Two people who thought, each in her own way, that she'd be different. The secret is neither more nor less than this, the two of them, here.

Chess rises, with some effort, from the broken chair, which offers a squeal of wood pressed onto wood.

"Made it," Chess says.

"I could really have that chair fixed. It's Shaker."

"This is not a Shaker chair. This is just a regular broken old chair."

"Still. I got it for almost nothing at a flea market."

"Just throw it away. Some things aren't worth the trouble. Even if we got them for almost nothing at a flea market."

"I suppose you're right."

"I think I hear Odin."

"It's time to go back."

"Everybody's waiting for us."

"Mm-hm. Everybody is."

Before they go back inside, Isabel checks Robbie's last post. There are forty-seven Likes.

Robbie has arrived. Outside Violet's window, he's a lesser darkness within the dark. He's a quickening, a flurry of animate air.

Violet had expected him to look more like himself.

She can tell that he's lost and confused, neither afraid nor unafraid. She's glad to know that. He's a sleeper who's woken in the dark and can't figure whether he's at home or not, whether he should go back to sleep or get up and find out where he is.

She can't tell if he thinks she's part of a dream he's having.

She can, however, stand in the window in the yellow dress, the dress he bought for her on a day he applauded not only for the dress but for the girl she was, inside the dress. She knows how much he wanted to see her turn more and more into herself, how much he wanted to be there for it. Now he's a flurry of quickened air, outside a house he doesn't recognize, but he is, in a way, turning more into himself, too. As that happens, Violet can stand in the window, wearing the dress, to remind him of this world as he leaves it for another. She can do that, for him.

G arth's headlights illuminate nothing but the road and the trees until they shine, abruptly, onto Nathan. Nathan standing on the shoulder, blank-faced. Garth pulls up, lowers the passenger-side window. Nathan pretends not to see Garth, or the car, at all.

Nathan's hair is wet, plastered in strands onto his forehead. Garth says, "What's going on?"

"Nothing."

"Are you wet?"

"No."

"Get in the car."

"I'm okay."

Garth leans over, opens the passenger door.

"Get in the *car*."

Nathan mutely obeys. He settles onto the passenger seat, does not seem to think about closing the car door.

Nathan is soaked. Nathan is shivering.

"Shut the door," Garth says. Nathan shuts the door. The car's interior light blinks out. Garth asks, "What were you doing?"

"Nothing."

"Were you in the lake?"

"Let's go back to the house, okay?"

"You're freezing."

"I'm okay."

"I got a blanket on the back seat."

"It's okay."

Garth reaches back for the blanket. "It's just a baby blanket," he says. He holds the blanket out to Nathan, who doesn't accept it. Nathan sits silently, his arms folded over his chest. Garth can hear his teeth chattering.

Garth wraps the blanket around Nathan's shoulders. Garth says, "What. In the hell. Were you *doing*?"

"Nothing."

"You dove into that fucking lake."

"The water was really cold."

"Uh, yeah. You want to tell me why you did that?"

"No."

"What if we weren't going home, or anyplace, until you tell me?"

"I was trying to see a star."

"What?"

"From the water."

"You could see the star from land, right? You could look up and see it in the sky."

"I wanted to see it from the water."

"Why?"

"I don't know."

"Why?"

"Maybe I thought it'd look different. I know that was stupid."

"Not necessarily. Not, you know, categorically stupid. But okay, yeah, kind of stupid."

"I thought maybe if I could see it from there, from this place nobody ever saw it. I don't really want to talk about this, okay?"

"Not really. No. Not really okay."

Nathan, shivering, looks ahead at the headlights shining

onto the road. He says, "When I went in the water, I couldn't see it at all. The star, I mean. It was just really dark and quiet."

"I'm not exactly getting the picture here."

Nathan says, "I wanted to know what it was like."

"What it was like."

"You know."

"I don't know."

"What it was like to be the water. In the cold quiet dark."

"Why would you do that?"

Nathan speaks to the road, not to Garth. "I wanted to know what it was like. For Robbie."

Garth lays his forehead on the steering wheel. He says, "Why would you want to know that."

"I do. Want to know."

"You're a kid. You're a little boy."

"I'm tired of people treating me like that."

Garth raises his head from the steering wheel. He says, "You shouldn't even be thinking about this."

"Everybody does."

A wind-stirred pine bough brushes like a broom over the top of the car.

Garth says, "You didn't do anything wrong." He leans in toward Nathan. He smells of cigarettes and something meaty, like raw sausage. It's the first time Nathan has gotten close enough to Garth to know what he smells like.

Nathan says, "Don't hug me, okay?"

"I wasn't going to."

"You're not crying, are you?"

"Nope."

Garth levels his face at Nathan's. Garth is not crying. It's embarrassing for Nathan to have asked in the first place.

When Garth says, again, "You didn't. Do anything. Wrong," he might be delivering an opinion as if it were fact.

Nathan listens. He listens to Garth. He watches the road. At night like this, beyond the range of the headlights, the road might go on forever, without leading to anything but more and more of itself.

"We have to get you home," Garth says.

"In a minute, okay?"

"Why do you want to wait a minute?"

"I just do."

"I'm taking you home in exactly one minute."

"Uh-huh."

Before Nathan knows he's going to do it, he reaches over, takes a hank of Garth's hair in his hand, and holds onto it.

Garth doesn't move. It seems to both of them that there's nothing more natural than sitting in the car together, as Nathan holds a handful of Garth's hair.

The headlights shine into the road, with its scatterings of pine needles, its ruts and runnels, the silver glint of a crushed Diet Coke can, the ongoing rolling nowhere of it. Nathan thinks of the forests from the old stories, where wolves or demons or candy houses awaited the children who ventured there. In the stories, though—the ones Nathan remembers—the children always won. They emerged unharmed. Nathan wonders now if the stories failed to mention the ways in which the children had been changed. Who wouldn't be, if they'd shoved an old woman into her own oven or outsmarted a gnome who wanted to eat them or been pulled by a woodsman from the belly of a wolf.

C hess lies on the sofa with Odin on her chest, hoping that an interlude of quiet will help prepare him to go to sleep for the night. He shouldn't have taken a nap, this late. He is, however, a child who barely sleeps unless he's too exhausted not to. He's a child who barely sleeps or eats. He does not care for any of the usual pleasures, neither rest nor food. He loves Chess, he may love Garth, and he loves the blue rabbit, which he's holding by the ends of its long arms, wiggling it. Odin is confused, as Chess knows, by the ways in which others, except Chess, fail to realize that the rabbit is a living entity, that it's merely unable to move, or speak, on its own.

Odin says to the rabbit, "Where was everybody."

"Everybody is here," Chess says. "Everybody is right here."

Odin wiggles the rabbit more vigorously. The rabbit is glad to hear that.

Chess and Odin and the rabbit will find a way, with Garth. It's too late not to. It's too late for Odin to be told that his father is unknown and unknowable, even if Chess does accept the offer at Berkeley, if she moves across the country and raises Odin on her own.

Whether she goes to California or not, though, she is stuck with this, with a man who wants more than she's able to offer. She'll have to be, however unwillingly, part of a family that includes a father who's not quite up to it, whether he lives a borough or a continent away. A father who can't or won't put others ahead of himself. A father who'll disappoint, who'll be fatherly when it suits him, when he feels up to it. She'll do her best, year after year, to convince Odin, as he grows older, that his father means well, that he has his limits, and that it's best to refrain from expecting more of him than he's capable of providing, whether he's late picking Odin up from school or has missed his flight to California.

Chess can't remember whether her mother ever told her any stories like that about her own father (*He works very hard, He was so poor growing up, He doesn't always mean the things he says*) or she told those stories to herself.

It's too simple to compare Garth to her father, to dwell on the ways in which she seems to have found her father all over again, despite their differences in appearance and occupation. It's also too obvious to ignore.

"Then everybody comes back," Odin says to the rabbit.

"Yes," Chess says. "Then everybody comes back."

D an stands on the front porch, with the nocturnal chirps and hoots out there beyond the wash of the porch light. He takes the vial from his pocket, unscrews the lid, snorts a spoonful into one nostril and then one into the other.

Here, instantly, is that sparkle and under-hum, the sense of snapping into yourself like a hand into a surgical glove. People, most people, have no idea about this jolt of return. You're back, you're yourself again, the static has vanished from your inner radio.

He should feel guiltier about it than he does. He probably should.

But really. Try being him, without a little help. Try being happy, insisting that you're happy, with your hiccup of success, your body of invisible followers, only a few of whom were deranged. Try being endlessly patient and paternal in the aftermath of your second failure. Try producing three meals a day, every day, and teaching your classes. Try bearing unresentfully the fact that all your efforts—your buoyant self-effacement, the grocery bag that split, in the rain, in the middle of Fulton Street—have not saved you from becoming an embarrassment to your son, who might like you better if you'd been a bigger hit. Even your family likes you better if you're famous. For that matter, try asking if being famous would actually have made it worse—how many adolescent boys want their fathers to be rock stars, with everything it implies about what the kid has to live up to? Try asking yourself if your son simply *dislikes* you. Try managing all that while you get up early with the kids and go to work and come home again to make dinner and, after you've gotten the kids into bed, stay awake deep into the night to write more music. Try being someone who refuses to give up, in the face of all evidence. Try sleeping four or five hours a night. Try being here, in this godforsaken place, where nobody seems to care that Robbie's death tore a hole in you too, where you're called on to help the others through it—part of the job, but still. A place where it would seem that you and only you know that you, in your way, have been as much widowed as anyone.

One more hit. Two more. The snap and the shimmer again, that much more so. Blessed substance, that can scour away the regrets and the recriminations, reveal the promise that resides under the forlorn surfaces.

And there is, after all, the promise of a renewed future with Isabel, the mending that's already underway. He's made dinner tonight, when she wasn't able to. He's poured wine for her, talked to her about how the children are going to survive this at least relatively undamaged. Those are small enough gestures, in and of themselves, but they speak beyond themselves.

There's that brightness. At the moment, he can see what awaits. Isabel will move back to the city. Their love, having survived its tests, will be stronger than ever. He'll keep writing songs, and this time he'll find an audience that won't drift away. If he's learned nothing else, he's learned that an artist is someone who refuses to listen to reason. Look at Garth, with a piece at the goddamned Whitney, after all those years trying to sell his work in second-tier galleries. Dan will keep at it. He will be on stages again, singing into the crowds. He'll no longer be an embarrassment to his son. He'll no longer be dismissed by mothers with jobs in finance.

All that unfolds before him. The healing has begun. He takes one more hit, puts the vial back into his pocket, and stands listening to the whirrings and buzzings of the night.

On the road in the woods, Garth puts the car into gear and drives, looking for a place to turn around.

Garth says to Nathan, "You're going to have to talk to your parents about this."

"I know that."

"You wanted to know what it's like to be dead."

"Not really. Not exactly that."

"Have you ever talked to them about it?" Garth asks.

"Kind of."

"You talked to me about it."

"I'm not *talking* to you about it. You just . . . drove up—"

"But we're talking about it. We're talking about it, right?"

"I guess."

"You can tell me anything, I'm here."

Garth is feeling self-congratulatory. Okay, if that's what he wants.

Still, Garth is here, as he says he is. Still, Nathan took hold of Garth's hair, he just *did,* he didn't say anything about it, and Garth didn't mind him doing that.

Violet waits at the window until Robbie's shadow has passed.

Robbie has seen her seeing him, wearing the dress, but she knows that he's less able, already, to tell the house from the woods. She knows he's fading into a place where houses and forests, where lights and the absence of lights, are all the same. She whispers, "Goodbye goodbye goodbye." She turns from the window to the mirror her mother has put here for her, an old oval mirror that stands on spindly metal legs, its glass clouded in the way of the worn-out things her mother favors. Violet stands in front of the mirror, admiring the slightly blurred image it returns to her, herself in the yellow dress.

sabel passes quietly through the living room so as not to disturb Chess and Odin as Chess whispers to Odin, "Look, here comes everybody."

Tomorrow they'll scatter the ashes in the less-than-ideal spot the children picked out, which will matter only to them but will matter to them. They'll return to the cabin. They'll pass the remainder of the day somehow, and then everyone will go home again, everyone but Isabel, who *is* home. She can't tell how long she'll remain here, but it'll be long enough to replant the garden in back, to fix the wobbly porch step, to have the broken chair taken away. To walk, most days, to the lake. It feels necessary to restore the cabin to some semblance of order before she moves on.

Once she's ready to leave here she'll quit her job, and find another. She'll figure out where to go next, how to relive her life with half-time custody of the children in whatever apartment she finds, which will not be easy, given the prices, but she'll find a place and it will be full of light and air, a place where the kids will feel comfortable and safe. She may—why wouldn't she—meet someone, at a party or at her new job or, if need be, on Tinder or OkCupid or wherever. She's looked already, though she hasn't responded to any of the inquiries. Still. There are nice-looking men, men who aren't young (she has no interest in younger men) but who are handsome and kind-looking. Who are, or appear to be, as ready as she is to forget whatever mistakes they've made and start again with someone else.

There's a life for her. She won't live on unimpeded. Some of the damage can't be undone, but she'll live on. She might be happy at odd moments, and maybe for longer than that. It strikes her as possible. It'll be up to Dan to find his own way, by himself. She wants him to be happy too, she does want that for him, but there's not much she can do for him, anymore.

It's time to go upstairs and call the kids to dinner.

She pauses at the foot of the stairs. It's time, no denying it, to get on with the usual business. She wants, however, to send out one more post from Wolfe.

She chooses a photograph she's been saving. A selfie. Robbie stands in the doorway of the cabin, smiling. He must have taken the photo in late afternoon. He's bathed in slanted golden light, the light that makes all of us look like the most burnished possible incarnations of ourselves. Robbie's hair needs cutting. He's wearing the Ramones T-shirt Dan gave him. He stands rakishly in the open doorway. Barely visible behind him is the cabin's interior—you can see a calendar pinned to the far wall, the corner of a bed piled with blankets, and the V of the fox's skull, nailed to the wall beside the bookshelf.

It's time for Wolfe's final post, before Isabel calls the children down. Before dinner and sleep, before tomorrow morning, when they'll carry the box to the shore of an unremarkable lake and say whatever there is to say (they've agreed not to prepare eulogies); before they come back for breakfast and fall into spasms of mortified laughter—*What are we supposed to do with the empty box?*—before it all goes on, tonight and tomorrow and the following day.

She posts the picture, Robbie in Dan's shirt, paused in an attitude of shy flirtation at the threshold of the cabin, as if small marvels awaited within.

> Caption: This is my last one, I'm signing off. It's the end of This and the beginning of That. Thank you for wanting to know. Right now it's what we call the incandescent hour when inside this cabin everything is lit like it's holy, including the tea kettle and the calendar on the wall. We're going to put some of this light in a jar, to take away with us. OK we know we can't get light into a jar but we're going to hold the jar up to the sky and screw the lid on tight and bring it home. We'll keep it sealed forever. We'll take it with us everywhere. Goodbye from this bright high place. Here there's something I can only call immaculate, some state of sacred suspension, but soon it'll be time to come home again, and go on from there. It's almost time now.

Acknowledgments

I find it difficult to refrain from acknowledging a considerable number of people, from Miss Janzen, my first-grade teacher, who persisted in the conviction that learning the alphabet would prove helpful later in life, to Pete Steres, my best friend in junior high, with whom I lived only ostensibly in suburban Los Angeles but more truly in Tolkien's Middle-earth.

I don't mean to be overly romantic. I mean only to acknowledge the fact that multitudes, throughout a writer's life, have inevitably helped, in a multitude of ways, to produce a novel.

More specifically, my boundless gratitude to Andy Ward, my editor. As editors go, incisive readers and stern taskmasters are increasingly hard to find. Thank you, Andy, for being both, for caring so ardently that a novel be the most potent, precise, far-reaching possible version of itself, and for being almost always right.

Frances Coady is not only the literary agent of my wildest imaginings, she's a brilliant reader, a confidante, and a friend. Frances saw this book through more changes than I care to remember, and never lost patience or heart. Whether she likes it or not, this book is almost as much hers as it is mine.

Bonnie Thompson, my laser-eyed copy editor, saved me from countless embarrassments, from questions of punctuation to matters of fact. I remain in awe of her capacity for attention to particulars, whether it's the difference between a semicolon and a dash or the fact that, although poetic license always wins out, there was, actually, no moon in the Brooklyn sky on the night of April 5, 2019.

My gratitude to those who read early drafts, and made invaluable suggestions: Ken Corbett, Marie Howe, Francine Prose, and Sonia Feigelson. For the last four years, Sonia's uncompromising intelligence, along with her organizational capabilities, have literally kept me afloat.

While writing this book I was surrounded by friends whose fascination with literature, whose pure love of it, helped produce an atmosphere in which writing a novel seemed, in theory at least, a plausible human act. Their faith often outmatched my own. Thank you to Amy Bloom, Susan Choi, Marcelle Clements, Hugh Dancy, Claire Danes, Richard Deming, Anne Fadiman, Jonathan Galassi, Meg Giles, Yen Ha, Courtney Hodell, David Hopson, Billy Hough, Sarah McNally, Christopher Potter, Sal Randolph, Marc Robinson, Nathan Rostron, George Sheanshang, Fiona True, Nina West, Leslie Wilder, and Ann Wood.

Among the most significant gifts anyone can offer a writer is a period of uninterrupted time. Thank you to the Fundação D. Luís I–Centro Cultural de Cascais, particularly Filipa Melo and Salvato Telles de Menezes. Thank you to the Santa Maddalena Foundation, whose director, Beatrice Monti Della Corte, is not only an inspiration but an intimate lifelong friend.

Thank you to Evan Camfield, who put up with my endless niggling over words, phrases, and fonts; to Lucas Heinrich, who created the beautiful cover; and to Richard Phibbs, for an author photo in which I look considerably better than I actually do.

My students at Yale University have proven, year after year, to provide a critical link between life as lived and the attempt to do justice to it using only language, ink, and paper. The privilege of conversing regularly with remarkable younger people helps keep the act of writing and reading feel vital and critically important, a conviction that does not necessarily accompany a writer every hour of every day.

I've had the good fortune, all my life, to be encouraged by my family. Thank you to Don Cunningham, Dorothy Cunningham, and Kristie Clarkin.

Nothing would be possible, not this book or anything else, without Ken Corbett.